Blood
Ain't Thicker

Holli Tabren

All rights reserved. No part of this book may be reproduced or transmitted in any form or by any means electronic or mechanical, including photocopying, recording, or by any informational storage or retrieval system without written permission by the author. Request for permission to make copies should be emailed to holli@hollitabren.com

This is a work of fiction. Any references or similarities to actual events, real people, living, or dead, or real locales are intended to give the novel a sense of reality. Any similarity in other names, characters, places, and incidents is entirely coincidental.

Text copyright © March 2023 Holli Tabren

All rights reserved.

Printed in the United States of America

1st edition

Copyright © 2023

All rights reserved by Holli Tabren

Visit my website www.hollitabren.com.

ISBN- 13: 9798377447283

DEDICATION

Have you ever met someone who gave breath to vision, or your encounter with them will forever be etched on your heart? Well, that's whom this book is dedicated to, God, and my friends Mary Worsley, and Timothy Moore aka the Tony Starks of the hood. Thank you for helping me see beyond what I could see. God, thank you for affording me the opportunity to experience their energy, I guess heaven couldn't wait for them.

CONTENTS

	Acknowledgments	i
1	TIME & TRUTH	Pg 1
2	FAMILY & FRIENDS	Pg 7
3	RHYTHM OF LIFE	Pg 16
4	BOUND BY BROKENNESS	Pg 35
5	THE WOUNDED NOW WOUNDS	Pg 59
6	LOVE & HATE	Pg 84
7	DREAMS & NIGHTMARES	Pg 130
8	SECRETS & SINS	Pg 139
9	MURDER-CYCLE	Pg 161
10	CHOICES & CONSEQUENCES	Pg 176
11	THE PLUG'S PLUG	Pg 181
12	VISION	Pg 189

ACKNOWLEDGMENTS

Lord, thank you for blessing me with the ability to speak and write in pictures. Your seed of promise allowed me to produce this literary product. I want to thank my parents William and Joanne, who helped cultivate my literary expression by equipping me with an array of educational tools. I want to thank my brother Lushan and my sister Lillian for putting up with their spoiled brat baby sister and allowing me to witness what overcoming looks like. Briangela, you're my favorite girl. Thank you, Tammie, for showing me the true meaning of friendship. D from the B, you already know what it is. I would like to thank Mrs. Jerlean Noble and Mrs. Rosa Bennett of the Columbia Writers Alliance, who told me from the moment we met that I was going to be an author. The social currency that I have been stacking up from our first interaction is unfathomable. I want to thank all my ladies at Camille and Leath, I'm making the pathway easier so when y'all touch down it's up. Big shout out to my family, my hometown Harlem, New York, and my second home South Carolina.

CHAPTER 1
TIME & TRUTH

A nonspatial continuum that is measured in terms of events that succeed one another from the past through the present to the future. (Time)

All truth is God's truth no matter where it is found.

(Clement of Alexandria)

All my life I was taught about the importance of time. I was told that it waits for no one, and it is not on your side. But is it? My parents use to say, make the most of your time because once it is gone you can never get it back. My favorite one was in time all things will be revealed to you good and bad. There was a profound sermon preached where time was used as an acronym for Totally Independent of My Existence.

As I sat in the courtroom awaiting judgment, I reflected on how much time I wasted and invested in activities and people that were no longer a part of my life now that I might be doing time. Am I a failure facing 25 years for drug trafficking, is my life over? How could I have let things get to this point? Admittedly, I allowed my lust for money and desire for material things to outweigh the plans that God had for my life. The OG's tried to warn me that the money was more addictive than the drug. Regrettably, I had been dancing with the devil far too long and my feet were getting tired, but instead of switching partners, I just changed shoes and got comfortable in my mess. Did I let the devil win? Was it too late? These questions run a continuous cycle in my head, however, what I did know is my family did not deserve the pain I was putting them through. Heartbreakingly, members of my family decided to take the stand and testify against me.

"Why have you decided to testify today," the prosecutor asked my cousin, Black.

Black's response astounded me as he looked dead in my eyes and said,

"Because the truth will set you free."

I asked myself, *how could he quote scripture (John 8:32) when his testimony was based on minimal truth mixed with many lies? How did I know that scripture?*

I was not as firm in my faith as I am today, but then

BLOOD AIN'T THICKER

I remembered a seed was planted that will soon be watered. Did it set him free, or lock him into a lifetime of snitching?

Afterward, my cousin, Lighty, took the stand with his mother, Blue, present in the courtroom. His whole demeanor was different from Black's, mainly because he used to live with me and the lawyer who instructed him with his testimony, I paid for. He could not look me in the eyes and tried to avoid looking in my direction throughout his testimony. Lighty's betrayal was the hardest and most lethal blow. His repugnant mother was more repulsive with her constant interruptions during the court proceedings. So much so, that the judge threatened to remove her from the courtroom. It is funny how people pretend so well. You see, while we were out on bond for three years I paid for lawyers, commissary, child support, and even transportation. If you were in that courtroom, you would never believe that there was ever any love or loyalty amongst our family. To Lighty's credit, once he got on the stand, he tried to change his story, but it was too late. He had already written a statement that was read aloud contradicting everything he was currently professing.

Initially, when my lawyers told me that my cousins were testifying against me, I thought that the prosecution was just trying to sow seeds of division. You know, like in every gangster movie where they infiltrate the organization and present one party with a witness list that shows that the other is snitching just to impart doubt. Next, the interrogated emotions take over and they start running their mouth because they were never as solid as they claimed to be. Then once they are done spilling out all the things the interrogators knew nothing about, they look up and the detectives have this big smirk on their faces like, got you! We had history, they were my big cousins who always protected me, I did not care what paperwork they showed me, it was a lie. Plus, Black made a deal with someone I had never seen before. In addition, Black and Lighty both claimed to have gone to school with the man and cosigned on his street credibility. So being that their misjudgment of character got us into this mess surely, they would take full responsibility. Regardless of what the prosecution said, I was sticking to my story. It took the wisdom of the

BLOOD AIN'T THICKER

elders--my momma, to help me understand that the cousins I held in my heart were different men than the ones on that stand. Their protection was seasonal, but their betrayal would last a lifetime. And I will soon realize that this whole ordeal would divide the family forever.

Philosophical education teaches that truth is subjective and solely based on one's belief, no truth is absolute. It amazes me how an individual's belief system is cultivated by the truths of their experience. My environment taught me that two sets of laws exist, the laws of the land and the laws of the streets. The order by which you abide these laws determines how your story ends. Was this the end? I was being judged by the laws of the land and felt time slipping away from me because the truth they wanted would have violated the code that I abided by under the laws of the streets. You may not understand, but there is a moral code in immoral actions. I had a contractual obligation that my integrity refused to amend by tearing someone else's family apart. My name is Hydessah Green and if you want to know what my truths are built on, we will have to go back, and after

HOLLI TABREN

being sentenced to 25 years, I got time today.

CHAPTER 2
FAMILY & FRIENDS

Family should be built on a firm foundation fortified by friends.

(Holli Tabren)

The sensation of the smoke I inhaled triggered a memory that teleported me to the rooftop of St. Nicholas projects where I first held the tube-like, hair-trigger, piece of steel that had explosive power. In the midst of loading the clip, loud banging snapped me back to reality.

"Who is it?" I shouted in response to the incessant knocking at the door.

"My Dessah, what are y'all doing in there?" Questioned baby girl in the sweetest tone.

"Briangela we are doing homework, and I will be out in a few. Has the movie ended?" I asked.

"Not yet, I just suddenly felt hungry."

She replied.

I instantly looked at my crew wide-eyed hoping that she didn't catch a contact through the door from the homework we were smoking.

"Okay, sweetie we will get something to eat shortly."

Dating older men came with big banks, blessings, and bonuses. One of my greatest blessings was being a bonus mom. But at just 16, what could I really teach her when I was trying to figure out this game of life myself? My superficial seductions and immaturity limited the value I could add to Briangela's life, and I knew in my heart that baby girl deserved so much more.

"I think she got the munchies," Empyreal teased.

"I know right, could that happen?" I pondered.

"We put towels under the door and the window is cracked, no way she caught a contact." Myangel chimed in.

BLOOD AIN'T THICKER

"This is some chronic though" Rykyia joked.

On cue, the room erupted into laughter with all heads nodding in agreement.

"When did she start calling you my Dessah," Angel asked.

"Girl one day she just woke up possessive acting like her daddy."

That comment amplified the laughter in the smoked filled room that was trying so desperately to cease. Stone had the best weed in town. People came from all over to indulge, rappers, actors, dignitaries, you name it. Back then it was all about Arizona, Chocolate, and Hashish. Every now and again some Dro would flow, but nowadays you can't even pronounce all the exotic labels of weed. Dating such a resourceful gentleman kept my pockets fat and duffel bag full. In addition, he purchased many of my first such as a car, expensive jewelry, and a pistol. Since my motto was "go big or go home" a TECH 9 was fitting. It was all Gena Davis' fault in *Long Kiss Goodnight* after her alter ego Charlie put that H-S Precision Take Down together with ease, I was hooked. Since I couldn't get the H-S, I had to start small, but big, you know. Unfortunately, my TECH 9 toting days were short-lived when my momma decided to shake down my bedroom. She whooped my ass for what seemed like hours, taking breaks in between to catch her breath. Promising the beating would end abruptly if I just told her who gave me the gun, but as she stared into my defiant pupils, she knew I would never tell. Tears welled up in her eyes as she said,

> "Why would you endure so much pain? Just tell me dammit."

As I digested my mother's disgust for me at that moment, I whispered to my soul,

> "If this is the consequence of the choice I made, then pain would be my portion."

Biennial family reunions were the highlight of the summer and this year we were kicking it

BLOOD AIN'T THICKER

off in the city that never sleeps. I phoned my cousin Que to get their location in preparation for tonight's events.

> "Heading across the George Washington Bridge, be there in 20 minutes," he replied.
>
> "Roll up Kyia, you know they have been sober the whole trip riding dirty so they can't wait to light up."

Ever since I touched that TECH, I kept a pretty pistol and was anticipating the new toys coming across the Turnpike. Thankfully, my parents were out of town for a few days and my brother wasn't getting back from college until tomorrow. We didn't need any distractions while disposing of these guns. If I had done a DISC assessment at that time, I was certain I would have been a high D. I was with all the smoke and never afraid to take risks. Reflecting on that night of the shake-down, my mother admonished

> "You think you know some gangsters, but I know the original gangsters. The survivors of death or prison are now presidents,

politicians, and preachers. The game doesn't change sweetheart, just the players. Remember that."

Then there was my brother Luch's voice,

"Granted you're book smart, but you're not prepared for these streets. It's a different kind of darkness out here that hides even in the light."

Later I learned that when the devil dangles all you desire, he never tells you that your decisions affect everyone connected to you.

When that beat dropped, the crowd went crazy.

"The concrete jungle where dreams are made of there's nothing you can't do, now you're in New York. The streets will make you feel brand new these lights will inspire you, let's hear it for New York, New York, New York."

BLOOD AIN'T THICKER

Jay Z and Alicia Keys' hit song *"New York State of Mind"* was blaring through the speakers as we entered Club Speed 30-deep. Seven ladies and 23 men headed to the VIP section to get the bottles flowing. Aside from my female cousins out of Brooklyn, there were very few women in our age bracket. So, we grew up around overprotective men who didn't play about their little cousins. My handsome squad drove the city girls crazy, especially with their deep southern panty-wetting accent. Within an hour they had their line up for the last few days of their trip, giving no thought to the wives and girlfriends waiting at home. You would think that being predisposed to all the doggish games men play I would be fully equipped, but when it comes to matters of the heart you're never prepared. Although I was extra feminine, being raised in an environment surrounded by hustlers, killers, robbers, players, and gangsters cultivated certain characteristics that conclusively birthed my microwave mentality. Soon I would learn that anything worth having is not easily attained. With six generations of cousins, you develop a significant bond with those more age-appropriate whom you entertain on a regular basis. Two of those men were Lighty, who resided in New York at the time, and baby-making Black who lived in South Carolina.

> "Dessah, you need to bring some of this chronic down south,"

Black uttered while trying profusely not to cough his lungs out after taking a pull of the grandfather blunt stuffed with nearly an ounce of chocolate.

> "Say less, we can make that happen. In the meantime, put that garbage you brought up here back in your pocket ain't nobody smoking that," I jeered.

The night was so lit, I loved partying with my family and friends. Angel was distracted drooling over this Brooklyn dude partying in the section next to us. He was checking her out all night as well, so the feeling seemed mutual. As the night ended Angel and I headed to the bathroom one last time hoping to run into the other ladies on the dance floor who had been gone for the past hour. Angel followed closely behind me Nectar bottle in

BLOOD AIN'T THICKER

hand, determined to finish it before we exited the club. Just before we reached the bathroom some bold-ass buster decided to grab my ass. Not just grab, this bastard cupped it with both hands, without a second thought Angel cracked him across the face with the Moët bottle and it was on. For a split second, I thought I was the star in my own action movie when my cousins dropped out of the sky like the rescue team, and pure chaos ensued. When the smoke cleared there were minor bumps and bruises sustained, but we left with everyone we came with, so it was a great night. However, I couldn't say the same for the others, there were plenty of bodies laid out on the ground.

CHAPTER 3

RHYTHM OF LIFE

Some say that the eyes are a window to the soul. Dejectedly, the image reflecting the person on the other side gets distorted sometimes. I wonder if the pain of the past is buried deep in the abyss of my soul.

Understanding my rhythm of life causes me to look deep into the eyes of the reflection in the mirror and pull out the pain buried within. (Holli Tabren)

Ascending the stairs of the brownstone, Myangel almost tripped walking through the door.

"Damn, could you cut on some lights? It is dark as hell in here."

Angel was a little curious as to the cloak-and-dagger feel of sneaking through the darkened interior. Yet, at the same time, the suspense turned her on. She felt Ty's fingers brush hers as his voice drifted toward her, he said,

"Take my hand and follow me."

BLOOD AIN'T THICKER

As they walked deeper into the dark Angel's eyes adjusted enough to make out a battery-operated night light affixed to a bedroom wall. Ty pressed it and the light gave off a pale amber glow, creating an illusory ambiance of romance. It was slightly dimmer than a candle, yet still served the intended purpose of minimal sight through illumination. Ty pulled Angel close and began kissing her passionately while caressing her body. She felt an instantaneous reaction as she moistened, involuntarily allowing a moan to escape her lips. She was entranced by the knowledge that this fine, sexy specimen of a man was about to make love to her. Ty licked her neck, whispering in her ear how beautiful she was and that he couldn't wait to taste her. Before Angel could regain her composure, another voice sounded off in her head. It was her best friend Dessah saying,

> "Be careful, you know them Brooklyn dudes be on some grimy shit."

Immediately the thought went to the back of her mind once she realized that she was naked, spread eagle with Ty's head between her legs. The sensation she felt caused her body to convulse unconsciously. When she opened her eyes, Ty was putting on a condom preparing to enter her. The feeling was like electricity shooting through her body, a mixture of pain and pleasure that only lasted about 3 minutes. Afterward, he stood up and exited the room without a single word.

Angel didn't know what to think, but possibly his inability to last longer embarrassed him. She made a mental note to stroke his ego when he came back--no pun intended. Noises from the hallway signaled his return, causing her to assume her sexiest pose. The door opened and to Angel's consternation, there stood a man she'd never seen before, holding his penis in his hand. She started screaming and he ran over, delivering a punch to her face so brutal it dazed her. Her eye began to swell instantly, and her friend Dessah's warning started to replay in her mind, but it was too late.

"Shut the fuck up!" he yelled.

As Angel glanced up, she realized there were four other guys, with no clothes on, watching from the doorway. He continued to beat her mercilessly. To add insult to injury he sneered down at her and said,

"Be a good little whore and play nice."

He raped her ruthlessly. The whole time he kept a sadistic smile on his face. Angel screamed for Ty over and over. Her only response was the jeering of the man grunting in her ear,

"He had his turn. It is our turn now!"

Ty never came to rescue her. She lay there going in and out of consciousness while one by one the rest of them entered the room and violated her in every orifice of her body. The last one to enter looked down at her broken, battered body. As he approached her eyes focused one last time, and from her lips two words that would follow him to his grave,

"Help me."

A barely discernible whisper was given with the last of her energy before her entire world turned completely black and she gave in to the fingers of unconsciousness which kept tugging at her fragile sanity.

The phone rang twice before Empyreal answered.

"Real, have you heard from Angel? Her aunt just called me worried sick saying she didn't come home last night. That is not like her."

Real was feeling the edginess creeping into her gut from the anxiety in my voice.

"No, what's going on?" Real asked.

"Well, the last time I spoke with Angel she was with Ty, heading to his spot in Brooklyn. She was supposed to call me when she got home. I never heard from her, so I assumed she got tired and forgot to call. Real, I have a bad feeling that something isn't right. I never trusted Ty; it was his eyes that told a different story from what was coming out of his mouth."

"Have you tried calling her?" She asked.

"Hell yes. A million times, but her phone

just keeps ringing and then going to voicemail. Even if she didn't call her aunt, she would have called one of us by now."

"Who is Ty, this is the first time I have ever heard his name?"

"The dude she met at the club a few months ago. Real, I am about to call the police. There is a possibility she can be tracked through her cell phone's GPS since it's still on. Matter of fact, I am going there personally, meet me at the 32nd precinct."

As I ended the call with Real, I prayed that Angel was okay. I dialed Angel's aunt, dejectedly reporting that she hadn't found Angel.

"Ms. Santos, I've called around and haven't had any luck locating Angel. Have you notified the police yet?"

Ms. Santos gave an exasperated sigh,

"Yes Hydessah, but they are downplaying

> the situation and saying she may be a runaway. So, I must wait 48 hours to file a missing person's report because she might pop back up. This is not like her; she is only 16."

I knew that words were useless in truly trying to console Ms. Santos.

> "I know, meet me at the 32nd precinct. I have an idea that might get the ball rolling."

I caught a cab to the precinct and paid the driver before he pulled up to the station. As soon as the cab stopped, I jumped out, screaming at the top of my lungs,

> "Help me! Oh, My God! Somebody, please help me! My friend is in trouble. You must save her, please!"

A crowd of police officers and court officials stood around talking. My sudden outburst prompted everyone to turn in unison and look in my direction. After a beat, one officer propelled himself into action.

> "Ma'am, please calm down and tell me

BLOOD AIN'T THICKER

> what's going on. Who's in trouble?"

Between hiccups and tears, I explained the situation.

> "My-my friend. Her name is Myangel Santos. Sh-She's only 16 years old."

The officer led me toward the entrance of the precinct.

> "Okay. Take a deep breath. We want to help, but to do that I need you to calm down so I can understand you."

I took a deep breath to steady my voice and began to lay it all out.

> "My name is Hydessah Green. My friend's name is Myangel Santos. She went out last night with a guy she met in Brooklyn a while ago. Everyone calls him Ty. She never came home and this morning there was a message from her on my cell phone. Here listen."

A voice emanated from the tiny speaker of the phone,

"Dessah, help me please-"

The message cut off leaving everyone hanging. I spoke up,

"I've been trying to contact her ever since, but the phone continuously rings and then goes to voicemail."

Real and Ms. Santos were standing behind me looking perplexed wondering how a message from Angel could be on my phone. Ms. Santos knew that the voice on the message did not belong to her niece. However, she did not comment on this, accepting that I had to take desperate measures to get them to act and look for Angel. So be it. She would find out exactly how I did it later.

The detective jotted down Angel's phone number and other vital information. With the help of her service provider in conjunction with the local phone company, they were able to triangulate the signal from her cell phone. Against protocol, I rode shotgun in Ms. Santos' car to the location. Real sat in the backseat praying in

BLOOD AIN'T THICKER

hopes that Angel was all right. As we reached the location, it seemed as though we could not breathe while waiting for the officers to tell us some good news, since we could not go inside.

As the officers entered the front door of the dilapidated brownstone, they immediately noticed that everything was eerily quiet, and it had the feel of being empty and abandoned. They began a thorough search of the premises, taking note of the lack of furniture or electricity. There was also a layer of dust that showed numerous footprints. The beams of multiple flashlights showed swirling dust notes stirred up by the onslaught of activity, giving credence to the thought that this place had been vacant for a while. Proceeding with extreme caution, they approached the back room, opening the door with trepidation of what horror awaited inside. It seemed pointless to even hope that the bruised and battered heap might have a pulse. The most hardened officer on the force found it hard not to shed a tear at the sight of the savagely beaten and naked body of Angel. The bed and surrounding area were covered with evidence of brutality: blood, feces, and condoms. The lead officer checked for signs of life and discovered a thready pulse. An ambulance was summoned immediately. The bed, a nightstand with a small radio, and an older model T.V. were the only pieces of furniture in the whole house. Upon further investigation, they discovered that there were no clothes, jewelry, or a purse belonging to the victim, anywhere to be found.

Inspection of the floor beneath the bed revealed a large crack between two of the floorboards. This is where Angel's phone had fallen. Her attackers had not seen this, or they would have been waiting on a coroner instead of an ambulance. Paramedics were ushered into the room, immediately going into lifesaving mode. They confirmed that she still had a pulse as they placed her on the gurney. Her only chance for survival was to get her to the hospital promptly.

As they exited the house with Angel on the stretcher, Ms. Santos, Real, and I began to wail. The officer approached us, offering necessary words of comfort and assurance that Angel was alive and what hospital she was being taken to. He told us to follow him,

BLOOD AIN'T THICKER

which would allow them to maneuver quickly through traffic. Upon arrival, we found the waiting room in pandemonium. Ms. Santos paced back and forth to the nurse's station with numerous questions. She was not going to rest until she got some answers on Angel's condition. Real and I tried to offer each other comfort, but we were emotional wrecks with bouts of venomous anger. This made it exceedingly difficult to think clearly. I battled with feelings of guilt, telling myself that there should have been something I could have done to prevent this from happening. I turned to Real with sorrow etched all over my young face,

> "Real, how could this happen? We were supposed to be there to protect her."

Although we were not blood, our bond was thicker.

> "Ty and whoever else is responsible will pay for this with their life."

Finally, the doctor emerged through the swinging doors of the emergency room.

> "Julia Santos, the doctor bellowed."

Julia ran straight to him,

> "How is my baby? Is she stable?"

The doctor wore an expression of intense dread at having to relate the severity of the patient's injuries.

> "Ms. Santos, Angel is going to be okay, but she has been severely beaten and brutally raped. It is apparent that this was a gang rape, as is evident by the presence of five different DNA types found on her body. Physically, she'll eventually heal. She will have a small scar above her right eye where we had to put five stitches. I suggest therapy to assist in her mental and emotional healing. In my experience, with most cases of this nature, girls her age fall into severe depression from the trauma."

Julia nodded her head in agreement. She knew that she would have to be strong for her precious Angel.

> "I understand, doctor. And I'll do whatever is necessary for her well-being. May we see

her now?"

"Yes, you may. The nurse will escort you to her room. Excuse me for a moment, I need to go speak with the detectives."

When they entered the room and saw Angel laying in the elevated bed they sobbed uncontrollably. Her face was so bruised and swollen. I looked at her and all I could say was,

"I'm sorry. I'm so sorry this happened to you. I should have been there."

Angel, through her own tears, reminded me that it wasn't my fault, and if I had been there the same fate would have befallen her.

Julia sat at the end of the bed, caressing Angel's hand.

She spoke from her heart,

"I love you, precious, and I am going to take care of you. We are going to get through this together."

Angel's face showed signs of anguish in her soul. She turned her head and stared out of the window; her eyes black as night reflected the emptiness in her heart. She then looked at her aunt with dead eyes and said,

"They should have killed me."

Her aunt was crushed to hear the dismay in her words.

"Don't say that. You have too many people here that love you."

"You don't understand, they overdosed me with pain giving me the propensity to never experience pleasure again."

At that moment the door swung open, and several detectives entered the room. One had an expression on his face that said he was serious about his job. He took the lead.

"I'm sorry to interrupt, but we have a few questions we need to ask Miss Santos so that we may be able to apprehend the perpetrators of this attack. For starters, who

BLOOD AIN'T THICKER

is Ty and what is his full name?"

To my extreme consternation, Angel replied,

> "I'm sorry but I don't know anyone named Ty."

One of the officers looked at me in confusion. My mouth was hanging open and my eyes revealed the shock at my friend's denial of knowing Ty. I wondered why Angel was lying. The detective continued his questioning.

> "Miss Santos, do you know who did this to you? How did you end up in that house?"
>
> "I don't remember anything," Angel stated.
>
> "What about the call you made to your friend, Hydessah?"

Angel looked perplexed as she said,

> "I didn't make a call."

The detective was trying to be empathetic, but his patience was waning when it appeared Angel was stonewalling.

> "Look, Miss Santos, I know you've suffered a lot of traumas, but the only way we can find these guys is if you help us."

Angel let out a pent-up breath in apparent frustration.

> "I'm sorry detective, but I don't remember anything."

The detective closed his notebook and slid it back into the inner pocket of his suit jacket.

> "Okay, Miss Santos, if you remember anything just give us a call. Here's my card."

He turned towards Julia.

> "Ma'am, may we speak to you outside for a minute?"

Julia stepped into the hallway with the detectives. As soon as the door closed behind them Real and I jumped up to get answers.

> "Angel, why did you lie to the detectives?"

BLOOD AIN'T THICKER

I demanded as Real joined in,

"They need to pay for what they did to you!"

A transformation took over Angel's features and she vehemently spoke words that made goose flesh crawl over the forearms of both of us.

"Oh, they are definitely going to pay. I am going to package this pain and personally deliver each perpetrator their present. You couldn't fathom what those bastards did to me. I will not give them the luxury of going to prison for a little while only to get out and run the streets again. Hell no! They will beg for their life just as I begged for them to stop ripping me apart. I am going to immensely enjoy watching them suffer."

Real and I were stunned as we exchanged glances. Our friend's pledge of retribution left us speechless. Angel was filled with hate and rage. Everything she said sounded so sadistic. We knew this victimization caused a drastic change in her and whatever she wanted to do they were down with it. Real mirrored Angel's expression as she spat out,

> "That's right Angel, we're going to get all those bastards.

CHAPTER 4
BOUND BY BROKENNESS

"There will be times in your life when you will despise the reflection in the mirror; others when you can't imagine being anyone else." (Holli Tabren)

――――Five Years Later-----

I awakened in my parent's home to the mouth-watering smell of breakfast cooking. A smile spread across my face knowing that today was my day. I was now 21 and would be celebrating my birthday tonight.

No more fake IDs, I announced aloud looking at the fake passport I'd used for years laying on the nightstand. As usual, my mother was starting off this special day with a birthday breakfast. Before getting out of bed, I thanked God for allowing me to see another day, as well as my incredible parents. Heading towards the kitchen after freshening up in the bathroom, I passed my father who was in the living room. I threw my arms around his neck and delivered a quick peck to his cheek.

"Hey daddy, what are you doing?"

He smiled lovingly,

> "Hello, pumpkin. I'm just waiting for your mother to finish up breakfast and was about to come to wake you up so I could……. Happy birthday Hydessah"

He started singing the birthday song like he always did since I was a little girl. I always loved it when he sang to me. He had a wonderful baritone voice and used to be a member of a popular group called Odyssey. We both turned simultaneously at the sound of my mother's voice coming from the kitchen.

> "Honey the food's ready. Did you wake up Hydessah?"

> "Mommy, I'm up already. Here we come."

When we entered the kitchen, mommy greeted me with a kiss and a big hug.

> "See, baby, I told you 21 would be here soon enough. You young kids nowadays want to be grown so fast, but y'all need to enjoy youth because you are guaranteed to

get older every year, but you can never get younger."

I rolled my eyes playfully and said,

"I know Mama. Are you going to lecture me on my birthday?"

She could only smile,

"No baby. Here's your plate. Enjoy. You have a big day ahead of you. Honey, bless the table please."

After Daddy said the blessing, he handed over an envelope and told me happy birthday once again. I could hardly wait to finish my breakfast so I could see what the envelope contained. When I opened it there was $2000 and a set of keys with a keychain sporting the Mercedes-Benz emblem. My heart nearly stopped beating. Then excitement took over and I started jumping up and down.

"Daddy, where is it? Oh my God! Thank you, daddy!"

My father was elated at my joy.

HOLLI TABREN

"Calm down, pumpkin, it's right out front."

As I turned to go outside my mother said,

"My present is in the glove compartment."

I ran down the stairs and out the front door. My eyes nearly popped out of their sockets at the sight of the apple red CLK320 parked in front of the drive. When I opened the door, the freshness of the new car smell assaulted my senses, transporting me to fantasies of the places I would go and the admiration of my peers. Upon closer inspection, I realized that my initials were embossed on the headrests. Not to mention the peanut butter-colored leather interior. I opened the glove compartment, retrieving the card that my mother had left. It contained gift cards from each of my favorite stores, including a day spa and detailing shop. My parents were always on point, and I was ready to see what the rest of the day had in store for me.

Empyreal stood in front of the mirror putting the finishing touches on her attire. She admired the sleek cut of the

BLOOD AIN'T THICKER

Donna Karen pants suit she wore in royal blue with gold baroque buttons. The color of the suit next to her dark skin created a beautiful contrast that was reminiscent of a night sky at twilight. Around her neck lay a simple silver chain holding a filigreed medallion with a cameo inset. From her ears dangle teardrop sapphires surrounded by a diamond setting. Completing the ensemble was a pair of Manolo Blahniks, in the same shade as the suit, with silver accents that caught the light with each step she took. Rick entered the room and was awestruck at the sexiness that this vixen of his exuded.

> "Damn, baby!" He said, "You look good. Where are you going?"

Real turned around with a flourish, causing her long auburn hair to fan out and then settle in a cascade over one shoulder. She sashayed towards him seductively.

> "Dessah is on her way over to pick me up. Today is her birthday so we're going shopping and to the beauty salon. Remember I told you her party is tonight.

Are you coming?"

"You know I'll be there. How long before Dessah arrives?"

"She'll be here in an hour." Real said while looking at her delicate white gold Cartier watch.

"So-o-o…"

Rick began with a slight raise of eyebrows while suggestively licking his lips,

"We have plenty of time."

Real knew exactly what Rick wanted. It was as if he never got enough of her, and she loved the attention. As she finally completed the long stroll across her bedroom, she stood close to him and asked in her sexiest voice,

"Plenty of time for what, daddy?"

He was instantly aroused. She let her fingers dance down to his pants, caressing the bulge that threatened to break through the fabric. She felt his member jump in her hand. Real unfastened Rick's pants sliding them and his silk boxers down to his ankles. He stepped out of them, and she tossed them to the side of the bed. At the sight of his nakedness, Real became excited. And she kept her eyes locked on his as she fell to her knees and began to pleasure him. He loved watching her and it drove him crazy watching her watch him.

> "Real I love you so much, you are the best baby!"

His hips began pistoling back and forth as she felt his body convulsing ready to release. She stood up and slid off her pants revealing a lacy, white, Victoria's Secret thong. The wide-leg pants slid easily over her shoes. As she unbuttoned the jacket Rick's mind went into overdrive as he realized that she wore no shirt, only the bra that matched the thong, given the illusion of a camisole top. She unfastened the bra letting it fall to reveal her perfectly rounded breasts and enticing nipples. She eased her panties down and stepped out of them, never taking her eyes off him. By now she was dripping wet, and she couldn't wait to feel him inside of her. As she climbed on top of the bed, he motioned for her to lie down. He began kissing her passionately while stroking her breasts. He made his way up and down her body placing a trail of kisses everywhere he went. He suddenly stopped and stared at her. She was such a lovely sight to him, her smooth skin, and big beautiful brown eyes. She had perfect C-cup breasts, toned, flat abs, and an ass to die for. He yearned to play in her long, thick, satin hair. Real's voice snapped him back to the moment,

> "Baby, what are you doing? Please, Daddy, I want to feel you."

By then she began playing with herself. He loved when she begged. He was going to drive her crazy. So, he took her foot in his hand and began sucking her toes and she enjoyed every minute of it. He made his way up her body, and when he reached her sweet spot, she climaxed on contact. He continued until she begged him to stop. Complying to her screams for mercy, he lifted himself, stood over her, and began admiring her body, then he slowly climbed on top of her. As soon as he entered his personal wonderland, the doorbell rang.

BLOOD AIN'T THICKER

"Damn, baby, I know that's Dessah. Don't stop she'll just have to wait."

Standing there ringing the bell over and over, I began to ponder aloud, *I know she hears this loud ass bell*. She's never ready on time. Fuck it. I'm going to pick up Angel and come back for her.

I got back in the car and drove over to Angel's. Ms. Santos answered the door with a warm smile.

"Hey auntie, is Angel here?"

"Yes, Hydessah, come in birthday girl, and have a seat. She'll be down in a minute. Would you like something to drink?" She asked.

"No thank you. I'm fine."

"Oh, before I forget, I got you a little something. I hope you like it." Julia said.

"Thank you, Auntie."

Julia handed her a huge box with a big white bow

on top of it. Excitement was her expression at the sight of the box. She couldn't wait to see what was inside. Just as she was about to open it, Angel yelled,

> "Don't you dare touch that box until I get down there. I need to see your countenance when that gift is revealed."

> "Well, hurry up, girl you know I can't wait to see what it is," I replied.

> "I'm coming. Where is Real? I thought you were picking her up first."

I smirked,

> "That was the plan but when I got there, she didn't answer the door, so I came to get you."

Angel smiled knowingly.

> "She's going to be blowing up your phone in a minute. She and Rick probably had to get it in before she left. Okay, birthday girl, let's see what's in the box."

BLOOD AIN'T THICKER

Angel watched me intently as I opened the box. Immediately a huge smile spread across my face.

"Oh, my God! This is so beautiful!"

I screamed as I tried on the red and white custom-made waist-length mink jacket.

"Thank you, Auntie."

Angel, looking like the cat that ate the canary said,

"Wait a minute. Open my gift next," as she handed me another box.

Inside concealed a gorgeous pair of all-white leather Christian Louboutin thigh-high boots. They matched the coat perfectly, especially with the red bottom accent. I threw my arms around the necks of both women.

"Angel, Auntie, you two are the best ever!"

Angel pushed her away playfully.

"Enough with all that mushy shit. Let's get out of here."

"Hey," said Julia "watch your mouth."

Angel cringed at her aunt's firm yet loving admonition. Julia smiled at the two beautiful girls,

"You ladies have fun and be safe."

We hurried outside and jumped in the car, giggling the whole time. Driving towards Real's house, I thought about how great my day was turning out thus far. Angel was admiring the new car in all its glory.

"Girl this Benz is hot! You are spoiled rotten."

Sucking my teeth, I retorted,

"Whatever. You and Auntie Julia helped get me this way."

"Well, you deserve it. You have such a big heart. Turn up the music. Let's check out the sound system in this joint. This is my song!"

Out of the speakers came the number one song in the U.S., by Kelly Rowland featuring Lil Wayne, called, *Motivation*. Angel started whining her hips, popping her fingers, and singing.

> "Girl... Girl, I turn that thing into a rainforest. Rain on my head. Call that brainstorming."
>
> "Weezy is so hot! He and Kelly killed this track," said, Angel.
>
> "Turn it down a second, my phone is ringing," I said.

I answered and immediately turned to my softer side.

> "Hello?"

The deep voice that came across the line gave me butterflies.

> "Happy birthday, darling. What are you doing?"
>
> "Angel and I are on our way to pick up Real so we can hit the mall and head to the salon. You know it's a must to be A-1 for my party tonight."

Stone spoke in his West Indian accent, and I felt as if chocolate was oozing through the phone.

"I would love to contribute to that. Swing by the spot. I got something for you."

Hanging up, Angel teased,

"Damn girl. That must be Stone got you all cheesing and shit."

"You know it. Something about that man just drives me crazy. He got me all riled up right now."

Angel reached into her purse, "Well, here's a baby wipe. You know I stay with the freshen-up kit everywhere I go."

"Girl, you crazy! Call Real and let her know we're pulling up to her spot."

Angel craned her neck and said,

"Isn't that her standing there like she been waiting forever?"

BLOOD AIN'T THICKER

I slowed the car down.

"Yeah, that's her."

Real observed the car coasting towards her. With admiration she said to herself, *that's a fly-ass Benz. I've got to upgrade.*

The car was slowing down the closer it got to the house. Once it came to a complete stop, she noticed her girls in the car and began to smile. The passenger window glided down with ease, and Angel leaned out. Real looked over at me.

"So, this is you?"

"Yeah girl, Daddy bought it for me. Do you like it?"

"Like it? Girl, I'm loving it."

"Well, get in so you can check out the interior."

Sliding into the backseat, Real reminisced on her and Rick's little escapade. Afterward, she had to jump in the shower and freshen up. The steam had frizzled her hair, so she brushed it back into a neat ponytail. She laughed as she pulled on a pair of jeans with a fitted white tank top because her Donna Karan fit still lay in a wrinkled heap beside the bed. Now, looking at the casual attire of her girls she realized how much more suited this outfit was for traipsing through the mall.

> "Dessah," Real yelled over the music,

> "This whip is fire! I love the smell of a new car. Have you blessed it yet?"

> "No, but we will soon…. roll up," I replied, while maneuvering the smooth ride through traffic.

Angel turned with a sly look to face Real.

> "So why didn't you answer the door when Dessah came by the first time?"

Real bit her bottom lip,

> "Girl I was getting blessed my damn self. There's nothing like a little vitamin D to start the day off right."

BLOOD AIN'T THICKER

"I told you she was in there getting her freak on. I knew it!"

They all laughed at how they knew each other so well.

"I got to stop by Stone's spot on the Eastside right quick," I announced.

By the time Real had finished rolling the blunt, they were already at Stone's spot.

"I'll be right back."

I jumped out and ran up to the front door. Before I could even knock, the door flew open.

"Hey, birthday girl."

Stone was standing in the doorway looking fine as ever in his dark blue Polo sweatsuit, white ones, and a New York fitted, cocked to the side to top it off. He licked his lips while letting his eyes roam over her body.

"Are you coming in or are you just going to stand there?"

Looking over my shoulder at my girls in the car

and then back at the chiseled, bronzed god standing before me, my mind started spinning.

"Hold that thought, and give me one second," I told Stone.

Heading back to the car I laughed at myself for what I was about to do. Leaning in the passenger side window, I held out my hand.

"Angel, can I borrow that freshen-up kit?"

"Oh, hell no! I know it's your birthday and all, but we are not about to sit out here while you get laid."

"Look, I just need a little tune-up. I won't be long. I promise. There's a liquor store about three blocks down. Go get us a bottle and let Real make her famous mimosas. And pick up some more dutches. Twenty minutes is all I need, so drive slowly."

Stone noticed that the vehicle I drove up in was pulling away from the curb, as I sashayed toward him.

"Do you see my new toy?"

"Hell yeah, baby! That shit is tight. All we got to do is put some rims on it and you'll be straight."

"No rims on this one babe, I am going to keep it classic."

"Why did your girls leave? Without hesitation, I suggestively replied,

"So, you could give me my gift."

Like a magnet, our bodies drew together as Stone grabbed me by the waist and started kissing me while closing the door and simultaneously removing my clothes.

Stone thought about *how her moans drove him crazy. He loved everything about Dessah. She was sweet, aggressive, and spontaneous, plus he never knew what she would say or do next. That was the reason why he was so intrigued by her. He was willing to give her anything she wanted.*

Angel and Real entered the liquor store and placed their order.

"Two bottles of Moët Nectar and a fifth of Hennessy."

"Henny is not one of the ingredients for mimosas," Real teased.

"I know, it's for later so we can take a few shots while we get ready tonight" Angel replied.

"Where is the party at?"

A male voice asked from behind. Real immediately went into flirt mode while Angel paid for the liquor.

"My girl is having a birthday bash tonight at the 40/40 club."

Real turned up her mega-white smile. Angel was busy collecting her change as she spoke over her shoulder blade,

"Let's go get the dutches and some orange

BLOOD AIN'T THICKER

juice."

"Real that's a pretty name for a sexy lady like yourself. My name is Maine."

Angel almost dropped the bottles as she turned around and saw whom the voice belonged to. It was the face that had haunted her for the past five years staring back at her.

"He had his turn, it's our turn now. Be a good whore and play nice."

The words resounded in her head, getting louder and louder like the approaching whistle of a train through a long dark tunnel. Her palms began to sweat followed by heart palpitations, but she quickly snapped out of it and regained her composure. She was going to use this situation to her advantage. The paralyzing fear snowballed into destructive anger. Maine didn't even notice a thing as he looked at Angel and asked,

"What is your name?"

She replied with a cool smile, "Precious."

Real looked at her and immediately noticed the change in her friend's demeanor. Maine didn't recognize the Angel that stood before him. She had changed drastically over the years. The black hair was long gone. All he saw was a red-haired vixen with honey-blonde streaks that flowed like satin to the middle of her back. She was 20 pounds heavier in all the right places and she had an assortment of colorful tattoos riding her light skin. The hat she wore perfectly matched her jogging suit and aided in hiding her identity. Real sensing that her girl was ready to go spoke up,

>"Come on, Precious, I'm ready to get my smoke on."

>"Real," Maine called out before they walked out of the door,

>"If y'all want some good, good holla at me. I got that Kush."

>"Yeah right. Everybody claiming to have the best."

Maine flashed an iced-out grill and reiterated his

claim,

> "But everybody can't back up their word. I live right down the block. If you two want to blaze up before you bounce, just let me know."

Real only took a second to contemplate her love of getting her smoke on, before she agreed to partake in his stash.

> "Ah'ight. Wait right here while we make a pitstop at the store to pick up the dutches."

As they walked to the store Angel dropped the bombshell on Real.

> "That is one of the bastards that raped me."

> "What?" Real screeched, feeling rage take root in the pit of her stomach and travel to every nerve ending in her body,

> "I am going to kill that motherfucker."

She spewed these words while tightly gripping her purse. She always traveled with her ultra-accurate Glock

43 handy.

> "Calm down Real. I got this. We are going to his house like it's all good, then I got something special for his ass."

Real made the purchases, including Angel's addition of a box cutter and roll of duct tape. All the while, Angel's mind was in retaliation mode. The thought of killing him made her wet.

> "What is wrong with me?" she asked herself.

CHAPTER 5

THE WOUNDED NOW WOUNDS

They say time heals all wounds, but it can also split them wide open. Then the time will come to relieve the pain. (Holli Tabren)

Maine couldn't believe his luck. These two baddies were about to come to get high with him. Just in case they wanted to front on him, he was already scheming and decided to lace the blunt with angel dust and spike their drinks with ecstasy, hoping for a threesome. He was getting aroused just thinking about it and he licked his lips as he saw them approaching.

"Are you ready playboy?" Real asked with a sexy smirk,

"You don't live with your mama, do you?"

"Don't play me, sweetie. I got my own shit."

The whole time he was talking he was leading them up the block to his place. When they finally arrived, he opened the door and stepped aside to allow them access to his castle. Upon entrance, Real had to admit that she was truly impressed with the decor. The apartment showcased beautiful Italian furniture, unique art, lighting, plush carpet, and a huge flatscreen in the living room.

> "Are you sure we won't be unexpectedly interrupted; this décor appears to have a feminine touch?" Real asked.
>
> "I told you ma, I live dolo, plus I hired a female interior decorator."

Angel began to take note of the pictures adorning the walls. As she got closer and the images became clearer, her blood pressure began to boil. Her nightmares took shape in the photo of all six of the bastards who had gang-raped her, along with a few extras. They were at some kind of party, posing with bottles of champagne and a few pieces of arm candy surrounding them. Maine's voice slightly startled her as he drew near and said,

> "That's me and my crew at my man Ty's

BLOOD AIN'T THICKER

club in Brooklyn."

The very mention of Ty's name almost made her give in to the tears that threaten to escape from her eyes. She couldn't believe she had trusted him. She had always wondered why he did what he did to her. Angel blinked to clear her focus and regain control of her emotions.

"What's the club called?" She asked, not wanting to seem overly interested.

"Jackson's, it's right off Nordstrom Boulevard. Maybe I can take y'all there one night. It's always jumping."

"Sounds like a plan," Real replied looking at her friend.

She couldn't wait to murk this nigga. Maine walked over to his system and out of the speakers pumped 50 Cents' *Many Men*. He began to rap in a slightly off-key voice,

"Many men wish death upon me; blood in my eyes so that I can't see."

Real leaned over and whispered to Angel,

"Perfect song choice for the occasion, huh?"

Maine returned his attention to the two dime pieces that stood a few feet away from him. He asked with gallantry that totally contradicted his thugged-out appearance.

"Would you ladies like a drink?"

"Sure", Real said.

"Pass me the weed so I can roll up."

She started dancing seductively toward Maine, he enjoyed watching her sway her thick hips. She knew she was enticing him. He forgot what he was supposed to be doing. He reached into his pocket and pulled out a bag that Real immediately recognized.

"Precious, he wasn't lying. This is that Kush."

Real had him in such a trance he forgot his original plan to lace the weed.

BLOOD AIN'T THICKER

"Fuck it I'll just rely on the ecstasy in the drinks to get the job done." He reasoned.

After taking a few pulls of the weed, Real passed the blunt to Angel. She enjoyed the sweet smell of the Kush lingering in the air. She walked back over to Maine who was sitting in a chair watching them and asked,

"Would you like a lap dance?"

He nodded his head as she straddled him like a professional horseback rider and began to groove to the beat of the music. She felt his manhood rising. He was so mesmerized that he didn't pay attention to Angel easing behind his chair with the champagne bottle. Before he could react, it was lights out.

While the ladies were handling business I was *handling business.*

"Right there, Daddy. Don't stop. It feels so good,"

I purred as Stone filled my insides while hitting it doggy style. He reached out and grabbed a handful of my thick silky hair. He loved the way it felt between his fingers.

"Daddy, pull it a little harder."

I enjoyed getting my hair pulled. It intensified the orgasmic feeling I was having, and I knew I was about to explode any minute.

"Oh, shit daddy. I'm about to cum!"

That was music to his ears because he didn't think he could hold it any longer. Almost in sync, we exploded together.

"Damn!" Stone stated on an exhale, "the way you just put it down, I wonder, is it your birthday or mine?"

I could only laugh,

"You're so crazy, boy. What time is it?"

"Around 2." He replied.

"Look out the window and tell me if you see my car."

Stone walked over to the window and separated

the blinds.

"Nah ma, it's not out there."

I admired his toned body and chiseled profile, I could go another round but knew my girls would be back any minute.

"Let me go freshen up and get dressed. They'll be here soon. They must have known I needed longer than 20 minutes."

"You better hurry up and get in that bathroom before I tackle you again."

Stone reached behind him and palmed my moist curls while slipping a finger into the cleft of my sex. I playfully pushed him away.

"You're right. Let me get going or I will never make it out of here."

Meanwhile Maine regained consciousness realizing he was naked and restrained.

"Look Angel the sick bastard finally woke up."

Real sneered at the pathetic specimen of a man before them.

> "It's about time so we can get this over with,"

"What the fuck is going on?"

He tried to say but quickly realized his mouth was duct taped and all that could be heard were muffled grunts. Angel was getting ready to answer every question that was on his mind anyway.

> "I know you're thinking what is going on, right?"

He nodded his head in agreement, watching the two naked women parade back and forth in front of him. At the sight of their naked bodies, he thought that hopefully, they were into some freaky S&M-type shit. He soon realized that was not the case when Angel said,

> "Be a good little whore and play nice. Ty had his turn. It's our turn now! Do you remember saying that to me?"

BLOOD AIN'T THICKER

Angel stood in front of him with murderous hate-filled eyes. He started to squirm in his chair, remembering exactly who she was.

> "I know you remember, and now it's your turn to play nice."

As Angel walked over to the table to retrieve the razor blade she purchased earlier, Real pulled the Glock 43 out of her purse and hit him across the face with it. He winced in pain as blood started to gush out the side of his right eye.

> "Calm down Killa," Angel said with a slight chuckle,
>
> "I want him conscious so he can feel every pound of pain I have for him. Go get the alcohol I saw in the bathroom."

With no fanfare or warning Angel bent over and grabbed his penis slicing it off with one swift motion. He tried to scream from the excruciating pain, but nothing escaped through the tape but grunts and moans. Real returned with the alcohol, opened it, and poured it over the open wound. Blood was swiftly pooling under him and dripping to the floor beneath the chair. With his bloody penis in her hand, Angel grabbed the broom out of the kitchen, came back, and push Maine face down on the floor with his hands still tied behind his back. She wanted him to feel exactly how violated she felt, so she used the broom to stuff his penis in his anus. The sodomization complete, she stood back admiring her work. While uttering the death sentence

"One down five to go,"

She felt liquid trickling down her leg and extreme pulsating in her vaginal area. *I need a shrink, this is crazy,* she thought.

They cleaned themselves up moving quickly. Angel thought about Maine's plush furnishings and figured he probably kept a stash on hand.

"Real, check the bedroom and see if he got some bread in this bitch."

Entering the bedroom, she began a thorough search of the dresser and closet. Just as she was about to give up, she noticed two black nylon duffel bags sitting partially under the bed. She lifted them onto the bed, taking note of their weight. Sliding the zipper down she saw flashes of green and the scent that only money could generate. Her eyes lit up and she whispered,

"Jackpot!"

The bag contained pounds of Kush, money, and a few bricks of cocaine. Angel stood in the doorway with a smile on her face as she watched Real return the contents to the bag.

After exiting the bedroom, they quickly got dressed and wiped off everything that they had touched without even a glance over their shoulders, they left the apartment, leaving Maine there to die slowly. Real began to laugh,

> "Whew, fuck them mimosas, I need a shot of that Henny now."

> Angel seemed deep in thought and finally said to Real, "Hey, let's not mention our little escapade to Dessah until after her

birthday celebration."

"Well, you know how disappointed she's going to be about not being there." Real warned as they arrived back at the car.

"I know but she is going to love this money she's getting as a birthday gift after we count it up, then split it up. It's over $100,000 in there. I'll grab five to blow at the mall on our outfits. Now let's go get Dessah."

When they arrived at Stone's I walked out to the car and gave a questioning look to my two friends.

"Damn, if y'all had taken any longer to get back I was about to go for round two," I said getting in the car on the driver's side while Angel slid into the backseat.

"Have fun, ladies!" Stone screamed out from the doorway.

"We will," we replied in unison.

I blew Stone a kiss and said, "Thanks for the

tune-up. I'll see you tonight."

Angel leaned in between the two front seats and commented,

> "Damn, this Benz drives so smooth we almost forgot to come back and get you."
>
> "Light up, Real, and let's get the party started."

As Real was lighting up Angel snapped her fingers and said,

> "Oh, yeah, before we hit the highway, swing by my house. I forgot something."

I looked at her in the rearview mirror and said,

> "No problem. Just don't take forever. You know how you tend to get sidetracked."
>
> "Two minutes is all I need." Angel promised, "I'll be in and out. Real, pop the trunk."

I looked at Real suspiciously as she reached over

me to hit the button without a word. Peering through my rearview I saw Angel extract two duffel bags.

"Where the fuck did duffel bags come from?" I asked.

"Just a little something we picked up while you were getting tuned-up," Angel replied with a smirk.

"Don't worry," Real added, "you'll see what's inside later. It's a surprise."

At club Jackson's, members of Ty's crew were discussing current supply and demand.

"Breeze, you heard from Maine yet?" Drew asked.

"Nah son," Breeze replied, "he was supposed to hit me up three hours ago so we could go handle that business."

Drew shook his head and shoved his hands deeper into the pockets of his jeans while looking down.

"Ty is heated, blowing up my phone saying his people ain't get them pounds they've been waiting for." Drew stated.

Breeze knew the consequences of fucking with Ty's money. The last mishandled transaction ended in a bloody mess.

"We might have to go pay Maine a visit, he is fucking up business."

Drew scoffed and tried to lighten the situation,

"Knowing his freak ass, he probably laying up. Regardless, business before pleasure, his priorities are jacked up, and he ain't answering his phone for nobody." He said while trying to reach him one last time.

Breeze looked up and saw Ty advancing toward them with his no-nonsense demeanor. As Ty approached, he dapped them up and went in,

"Yo son, Maine got me vexed. Where the fuck is he?"

Ty asked Drew while Breeze shrugged.

> "I don't know, but Breeze and I are on our way to his crib."

> "When you get there holler at me. My people have been on hold all day."

Ty pulled out a black and mild and lit it while contemplating how he was going to handle Maine for not coming through. It was unacceptable. Ty was a businessman and his clientele side-eyed him when shit fell short. He never wanted anyone to think he couldn't run a tight ship. His street creds should never be questioned.

> "This clown got me missing bread. Handle that and get at me." He told Drew.

With a final handshake, he replied,

> "I got you. But shouldn't we swing by Frank's first?"

> "Yeah." Ty said thoughtfully, "I'll meet you there."

BLOOD AIN'T THICKER

The candles illuminating the room were slowly burning out, leaving the Japanese Cherry Blossom fragrance in the air.

"Just like that baby,"

Frank said lustfully while looking down at Trina, one of his many baby mamas.

"You know exactly what to do to keep a nigga coming back".

As he palmed the back of her head, guiding her mouth up and down his shaft, he leaned back and closed his eyes in ecstasy. Just as he was about to bust, he felt a stunning blow land across his face. He screamed out in agony.

"Ha, fuck!"

His words caught in his throat as his tears cleared from his eyes and he stared into the face of death.

"Shit! T-Ty," he stuttered "I was just about to call you."

He tried to laugh to establish camaraderie.

"Shut the fuck up, you bitch ass nigga!" Ty spat out viciously, "You have been ducking me for two weeks, but it's all good. I got something for you."

Trina looked at her son's father and felt kind of bad for him, but her money hungry ass only cared about self. The $10,000 Ty offered her to set Frank up was well worth his life; she at least, thought so. She was practically spending the money in her head as she watched Frank holding his face. Frank looked over at Trina and it dawned on him that she was totally unafraid. She was slowly getting dressed and checking her appearance in the full-length mirror as if nothing was going on around her. At that moment the realization hit him like a ton of bricks that she had set him up. Deep down he knew it was his own fault for being such a fucked-up nigga. His actions or lack thereof did not instill loyalty. He had never done anything for her or his son. He only gave her a couple of dollars here and there whenever she pleased him sexually. As for his son, he could care less about him. He had six other kids anyway and only took care of the two with his main girl. Staring into the barrel of the Glock 26, he knew that karma had come back to bite him. He looked over at Trina and yelled,

"You grimy bitch, you set me up."

She didn't reply; just smirked at him and walked out of the room. Ty drew his attention back when he snared,

"If you handle your business like a man no one would be able to influence your son's mother to get at you like this. On top of being a thief, you are a no-good father and don't deserve to take up space on this earth."

Ty said all of this through clenched teeth.

"Now where's my fucking money?"

"Be easy! I got your money, fam, but it's not here."

"Ain't no fam here, nigga. You fucked that up when you decided to run off with my product. Breeze… Drew… search the place.

I know this nigga got something up in here."

There was a thunderous sound as Ty cracked him across the face with the butt of the gun which instantly split his nose. He pistol-whipped Frank continuously with such fury. He couldn't believe that Frank would try to snake him as much as he lined his pockets for years. If it weren't for him, Frank would be the same broke-ass nigga he was seven years ago.

"We got it, fam!"

Breeze yelled from the closet. Ty temporarily paused the assault on Frank.

"I thought you said my shit wasn't here,"

Ty said while raising his gun.

"Y'all get it all together and make sure he ain't got nothing else in here. I'm tired of looking at this piece of shit bleeding everywhere."

With that, Ty put two bullets in Frank's head and made his way to the door.

BLOOD AIN'T THICKER

"Give Trina a couple of days to enjoy the money then kill her too. We don't need any loose ends."

"I got you," Drew replied.

"Breeze," Ty said "hit Maine up so we can put the paperwork together and handle that business. He better be straight or he can get it, too."

With that declaration, Ty exited leaving Breeze and Drew to clean up as best as possible.

Laying back in the massage chair getting my pedicure done I said,

"This is so relaxing, I really needed this."

Angel called over a passing attendant.

"Excuse me, could you please heat my water up some more? It's getting cold."

"Yeah, right, Angel! You just like that water burning hot. I don't know how you can stand it." Real, said playfully.

"You are too yellow to have red feet. But I guess they'll go with those red bottoms you copped earlier."

"Whatever!" Angel said, "Don't worry about me. Your only concern should be picking the best design in this place for those hammer toes. You better be glad those hot-ass Emilio Pucci's you're wearing tonight will camouflage those hideous feet."

"I still get them sucked on, so I don't give a damn what you think," Real countered.

I played referee and mediator by saying,

"Now ladies, let's not argue over minor imperfections."

Real's cell phone signaled an incoming call. She reached into her pocket to retrieve it, realizing who the caller was, she answered with a purr,

BLOOD AIN'T THICKER

> "Hey baby where are you? OK, I'm getting a pedicure right now. I'll stop by before I head home to get dressed for tonight, so make sure you don't have any clothes on when I get there. I've got a sweet surprise for you. Okay, see you then."

I listened to her end of the conversation and could hardly wait for the phone call to end before jumping in,

> "You are a freak. All that fucking you were doing earlier when I had to come back to get your ass and you still ain't satisfied?"

Real licked her lips suggestively while pressing her body deeper into the massage chair, let me tell you, ladies, something I love me some good dick and can fuck all day. I think I'm a nymphomaniac.

> "Even when I'm satisfied, I am not satisfied."

All of us burst into laughter at the histrionics of the character sitting before us. Even the nail tech had to join in. Real continued, plus I got a special surprise for Rick.

"Speaking of which," Angel queried, "when are we going to meet the infamous Rick?"

I interjected, "I thought I was going to meet him earlier. I'm sure that's whom had you occupied when I got there."

Real sighed, "He might not be around long enough for you to meet. You know these niggas don't keep my interest for too long."

"One day you're going to meet your match and get turned out like Dessah over here."

Real wiggled her eyebrows and winked at Angel. I had no qualms about agreeing with the truth that they spoke,

"You might be right. Stone got me wide open right now. I love me some him."

Real stated, "At least y'all open off each other and it's not one-sided emotions. Matter of fact, I'm surprised he not blowing up your phone by now."

BLOOD AIN'T THICKER

"You're right. Where is my phone?" I asked while rummaging through my favorite Alexander McQueen purse.

"I must've left my phone at his spot. I hope he hasn't left yet. I'll stop by there on my way home after I drop you off."

CHAPTER 6
LOVE & HATE

When your heart breaks, your soul shakes.

(Holli Tabren)

Pulling up in front of Stone's, I thought about how happy his presence in my life made me. Walking towards the door, I visualized myself in a gorgeous Vera Wang bridal gown flowing with each step, and a smile plastered across my face. Feeling completely naked without my phone, spotting his truck gave me a sense of relief knowing I would have many calls to return. As I raised my hand to knock, the door swung inward. Visions of the many crime dramas I'd seen began to play in my head and I saw Stone, lying motionless on the floor in a pool of blood. But what met my eyes couldn't have shocked me more. My heart stopped as he exited the house with a woman I'd never seen before. The look in the other woman's eyes as we met, let me know that she was surely more than a friend.

"Who the fuck is this bitch?"

BLOOD AIN'T THICKER

I asked, never taking my eyes off the female.

Stone stuttered, "Nobody, baby."

A five-finger imprint was left on his face for the obvious lie, "Don't play with me. There's a whole fucking human coming out of your damn spot, clearly, she's somebody!"

The female took on a sister-girl stance with her hands on her hips and her neck rolling,

"What do you mean I'm nobody, Stone? I'm pregnant with your baby, but I'm nobody?" She asked.

"You need to find a better answer than that."

"Bitch, stop fucking lying! And baby, this bitch is lying!"

He screamed trying to plead his case. I felt as if my heart was about to explode out of my chest. I'd never experienced pain of this magnitude, but I refused to allow a single tear to escape in their presence. Stone moved towards me and reached out a hand which I brusquely shoved away. He was such an actor,

> "I'm sorry baby. This bitch doesn't mean shit to me. I love you."

Ice grilling him I verbalized my only concern.

> "Where the fuck is my phone?"

I was still trying to recover from the pain in my heart showing a crack in the veneer. I felt like I was about to pass out. Stone, not wanting to give up easily, even when caught red-handed, replies,

> "It's right here baby. I was on my way to bring it to you when I realized you left it."

> I smirked and asked facetiously, "Is that right? Give me my shit!" Dropping all pretense of niceness. "Do you know how much I loved you? You fucking bastard!"

Stone recoiled from the venom of my words as if he had been snake bitten. Trying to make a recovery, he pleaded,

> "Baby I'm sorry. Please don't do this to me.

BLOOD AIN'T THICKER

She's lying."

I turned my gaze to the tear-filled eyes of the woman standing before me and my woman's intuition kicked in, telling me with certainty that this woman was telling the truth. She was just as hurt as I was. Returning my hate-filled attention back to Stone, the hate leaked into my heart and spewed out of my mouth,

> "Handle your responsibilities nigga, because we are through. And whatever you do, don't show up at my party tonight because I might put a bullet in your ass."

With this last declaration, I left him, and his heartbroken baby mama standing on the stoop hopped in my Benz and drove off. In the privacy of my car, the floodgates parted, and a few tears escaped, which I quickly wiped away. I felt my heart harden as if ice was encasing it like a sculpture, so I popped in my classic Lil Kim cd, lit the half blunt of Kush left in the ashtray, and looked in the rearview mirror, as I reached to crank up the volume, my phone rang.

"Happy Birthday my Dessah, I love you, when are you coming to pick up your present?"

Briangela's voice instantly transformed that sculpture into a slushy.

As Real approached Rick's condo, she thought about how much she enjoyed being around him. He always made her feel so good and she loved his head game. He knew how to put it down in the bedroom. Reaching across the seat she grabbed her multicolored Dior purse which enhanced her sexy sultry look. She stepped out of her white Cadillac Escalade, turning down the color of her purple leather catsuit adorned with 4-inch Jimmy Choo stilettos that matched perfectly. Heading into the building, she just made it to the elevator before the doors slid shut. As she reached her destination, she popped an altoid in her mouth, always making sure she stayed fresh between her lips the ones that speak and the ones that don't. After the first knock, the door swung open, and Rick greeted her with the biggest smile.

BLOOD AIN'T THICKER

"Well, hello sexy. What do I owe for this visit?"

She wrapped her arms around his neck and gently scraped her teeth against his earlobe. I just had the urge to see you before the party tonight. I don't have much time so fix us a drink while I make myself more comfortable. And I thought I told you to be naked when I got here. Sliding off her shoes, she looked around his condo and admired how beautiful it was. He had amazing taste. She remembered when she helped him pick out the Oscar Dela Renta set, from Century Furniture, which adorned his living room. Rick's voice drifted into her thoughts as he said,

"Here you go, Beautiful."

He walked from the kitchen with two glasses of Henny and Coke in hand. *Damn, she's fine*! Rick thought to himself as he watched her peel off her clothes, revealing a sexy lavender lace bra and panty set by Laperla.

"Put your heels back on baby." He

instructed.

He loved her in her birthday suit and stilettos, knowing that the panties and bra would soon be a distant memory.

"Come on, Daddy," Real said while sauntering toward the bedroom, "Bring the drinks with you."

She grabbed her oversized bag filled with all kinds of kinky toys. Sipping her drink, she watched Rick remove his clothes.

"After you're done, come take off the rest of mine."

She said while standing at the edge of the bed watching him get completely naked. She always admired his physique and loved to run her hands up and down his six-pack like a washboard. His chocolate skin tone was so smooth, and he had the most beautiful smile, with perfectly straight white teeth. She snapped out of her daze as he reached up and unhooked her bra. She finished off the rest of her drink and placed the glass on the

BLOOD AIN'T THICKER

nightstand.

"Mm-m-m Baby you smell so good".

He whispered as he inhaled the scent of her Jean Paul Gaultier perfume. He removed her bra, exposing her erect breasts, and bending to place them one by one, into his mouth. He circled her hardened nipples with his tongue, and gently bit down on them with a soft nibble. Real moaned with pleasure. She laid back on the bed and he removed her panties, revealing a fresh Brazilian. Spreading her legs completely open, his mouth watered. He cuffed her ass cheeks, so he had a nice firm grip, then proceeded to pleasure her immensely. Real was experiencing such bliss, she wanted to climb the walls. But his hold on her was so tight, she couldn't do anything but scream and moan until her whole body began to tremble. As she tried to catch her breath a single tear rolled down her cheek from the wonderful orgasm. Real sighed when she finally caught her breath,

"That felt so good, come here so I can return the favor."

I got some toys in my bag. Do you want to play? Rick got excited at the prospect and replied,

> "Hell yeah! You know I love that freaky shit."

First, she pulled out two sets of the furry handcuffs they use quite often and cuffed each of his arms to the bedpost. Then she grabbed the blindfold, placing it securely over his eyes. Not being able to see a thing his mind raced wondering what pleasurable feats she had in store for him. He loved her versatility and how she was always willing to try new things. Suddenly a glimmer of uneasiness came over him as he felt something slide into his mouth that almost caused him to choke. His body jerked at the intrusion. When the blindfold came off his eyes, he knew that something was totally wrong.

Real's look of seduction had been replaced by a scowl. He wanted to ask what he had done, but he realized he was gagged. As she began to speak, tears roll down her face. Not of joy, but of extreme sadness and hurt, because she thought she loved him.

BLOOD AIN'T THICKER

"I saw you today." She said simply.

He stared at her while searching his mental Rolodex, knowing that he hadn't been with anyone since he met her. She was more than enough for him to handle.

"You know, she continued I never paid a lot of attention to the photo in your living room until I saw it at Maine's house."

"Maine? What the fuck was she doing at Maine's house?" He thought to himself.

"Do you remember about five years ago when you and your boys brutally raped and beat a young girl name, Angel?"

He closed his eyes tight and reflected on that terrible night that had tormented him up to this very day. Hearing the young girl screaming for help, he knew what his boys were doing was wrong. He wanted to do something but was too scared to go against Ty. Once the others were done assaulting her, he was told it was his turn. Maine told him to grab all her shit when he got through and to hurry up so they can get out of there.

Once everyone left the room, Rick just looked down at the badly beaten girl who was saying,

> "Help me," in a barely audible voice.

She had opened her eyes briefly, then blacked out. He never touched her, he grabbed her belongings and upon noticing her cell phone, he placed it into a large crack he discovered beneath the bed, hoping that someone would be able to trace it and therefore find her before it was too late. Real brought him back to the present, screaming,

> "She is one of my best friends and you raped her!"

He would never get the opportunity to tell her that he didn't touch Angel, but it wouldn't have mattered because he did not stop it from happening. She looked at him through murderous eyes,

> "Just to let you know, Maine is already dead, and after I kill you, the rest of your crew will follow."

"Enough of the small talk, she said

BLOOD AIN'T THICKER

nonchalantly I've got a party to attend."

Wiping tears from her eyes while reaching for her purse, she extracted a surgical scalpel she got from a doctor at the Harlem hospital she used to see. She sliced off his penis with the precision of a surgeon, heedless of the screams muffled by the gag. She then slit his throat. When she was sure he was dead she removed the gag and placed his penis in his mouth, one last tear was shed for him as she cleaned up and left.

When I pulled up at Real's house I saw Angel's royal blue five series BMW and knew that the girls were awaiting my arrival. I sat in the car for a moment thinking about the altercation between me and Stone. No matter how many fuck nigga songs I listened to I couldn't ignore the feeling of my heart literally breaking. Thinking of my baby girl, I unconsciously reached for my belly. Although I didn't birth her, she had been in my life since she was three years old. Briangela was so much like me it was scary. Nearly six years later reflecting on her first day of school made my heart smile. Bri came home flustered with fury in her eyes and that day she decided to call me Ma, which she would interchange from time to time depending on her mood.

> "You weren't doing no homework, in that room, this is homework." She bellowed while holding up a folder containing her assignments.

At just five years old I learned a valuable lesson about her personality, you can't tell her just anything, she remembers everything, and will always speak her mind. Feeling a waterfall of tears cascading down her face she asked herself.

What do I do now? What rights do I have as a bonus mom when the relationship ends? None! I know one thing her grandmother better not call me saying he is slacking on anything when it comes to her.

Although he had other children, she was the only one who lost her birth mother at three months old. What would this do to her tender heart? I finally understood the

BLOOD AIN'T THICKER

definition of heartbreak as my hand subconsciously ascended from my belly to my chest.

Knowing I had to pull myself together before I went inside to prevent my girls from noticing the pain in my eyes, I wiped my face and grabbed a blunt in hopes that it would get the blame for these puffy eyes. I was determined to enjoy my party and inform the ladies of the day's events tomorrow. Unbeknownst to me, we all had a story to tell each other. Finally exiting the vehicle, I realized that each step taken felt weighted, the burden of emotions gave me a heavy bodily sensation.

"What took you so long to come inside?" Real asked as I walked through the door.

"You know the ritual, get the shot glasses ready."

I stated while admiring myself in one of the many mirrors scattered strategically throughout the house,

"Plus, the limo won't be here for another fifteen minutes. I would love nothing more than to drive my new toy, but Daddy made me pinky swear not to drink and drive."

The Roberto Cavalli red and black embroidered dress looked so elegant. Complimented by red Ferragamo calfskin pumps, along with my platinum Cartier jewelry that made me appear to be glowing with every step. We were determined to be the envy of everyone in the club tonight. After Real applied the finishing touches to her makeup, she walked out of the bathroom looking like a supermodel in her white Emilio Pucci long-sleeved crocheted dress that stopped mid-thigh. Her feet were encased in white, and gold crocheted six-inch heels to match. Her Bulgari jewelry enhanced her look and brought out the gold streaks in her hair. She lifted her shot glass into the air to make a toast, and the others followed.

> "Happy Birthday to the realest woman I know, who happens to be one of my best friends. You are the greatest, and I wish you many more."

The ringing of a cell phone interrupted the festivities as I reached into my Hermes clutch and looked. Seeing Stone's number caused my blood to boil, and I instantly turned the phone on vibrate. Then looked out of the window to see if the limo had arrived.

> "Don't worry, it will be here soon," Angel said.

I turned around and smiled looking at my friend.

> "Why are you smiling at me like that?" she asked.

> "Because you look gorgeous in that dress," I replied while camouflaging my true thoughts.

Angel executed a sexy spin, showing off her black sparkly Chanel cocktail dress with matching black Christian Louboutin. Her diamond chandelier earrings were all the jewelry she wore, but they made her whole look fantastically stunning. The sound of a horn blowing turned all our attention to the window.

> "Angel turned and said, told you to have a little patience."

HOLLI TABREN

Drew and Breeze pulled up in front of Maine's house,

"This nigga better not be up in here with no bitches." Drew said to Breeze, referring to Maine's sorry ass.

"Making us come all the way down here because he doesn't want to answer his phone," Drew said callously.

He knocked at the door several times.

Breeze declared. "Somebody's in there. I hear the music."

Drew got angrier with every second that passed.

"I'm about to go in on this nigga for being so slack."

He continued knocking to no avail.

"He acts like he doesn't want to answer the damn door," Breeze said as he reached down and turned the knob.

BLOOD AIN'T THICKER

To his surprise, the knob turned easily, and the door opened right up.

> "Damn! What the fuck is that smell?" Drew asked.
>
> "I don't know, but something is not right," Breeze answered.

As they made their way into the house, they stopped dead in their tracks and almost vomited.

> "What the fuck?" They said in unison.

Their brains couldn't think of anything else as they looked down at their mutilated friend. Drew dialed Ty's number to deliver the news.

> "Ty, we got a problem."
>
> "What kind of problem? That nigga better come correct with my shit." Ty threatened.
>
> "Well, Maine is dead. Somebody did him dirty, Fam. They fucking sliced off his dick and everything. He got a broom shoved up his ass!"

"Calm down. Search the place and see if whoever did this took the money and work, then get up out of there. I'll have someone call the police." Ty said.

"We searched the place from top to bottom. The money and the work are gone. It's strange that all his jewelry was still there, but I snatched it up." Breeze said.

Ty pondered aloud, "Who would do this shit?"

"I don't know fam," Breeze offered, "He wasn't beefing with nobody, but Stone over territory. Once we established that Maine would only pump the coke and Stone will still be holding down the weed everything was all good."

"What man would cut another man's dick off unless he was fucking his girl."

"So, what you saying? Do you think it was a bitch that did this?"

BLOOD AIN'T THICKER

Drew joined in the conversation.

"I don't know for certain, but a nigga wouldn't have left the jewels," Ty stated.

Drew added, "True that. Unless it was a bitch not really pressed for paper. Knowing Maine," he was probably flossing and since they were going to kill him anyway, they took the money and the work. It would be too risky to pawn the custom-made jewels he had."

"Nigga please, you need to stop watching CSI and criminal minds. Shit, you sound like one of them profilers," Ty said. "But you might have a point. Holla at your people in the streets and see if they heard something. We need to find whoever did this before the police do. If this turns out to be a chick, we need to be extremely careful, because she has already shown us that she is a ruthless bitch."

"Or bitches," Breeze picked up the thread, "it had to be more than one."

As I sat back, sinking into the plush leather seats of the stretch Hummer, while sipping on a glass of Rose', I thought about the close relationship I had with my girls and how much love I had for them. Wishing that Kyia was able to celebrate my special day with us, I felt incomplete. I missed her so much. After Kyia moved to South Carolina we saw less of each other.

> "What are you over there thinking about so hard?" Real asked.

Appearing downcast in spirit, I declared aloud,

> "I miss Kyia and wish she was here with us."

Real smiled and reached over to give her friend's hand an encouraging squeeze.

> "I know you do but we're going to visit her next week, and we can just celebrate again."

BLOOD AIN'T THICKER

"I guess you're right," she conceded reluctantly.

"Damn! What the fuck?" I screamed watching several police cars speed by.

They were mere inches away from sideswiping the limo. The high rate of speed that the cruisers were traveling at caused a wake of wind that slightly rocked the huge Hummer. The deafening screech of sirens and the constant stream of pulsing lights let them know that the NYPD was on a serious mission.

"Someone must've robbed a bank... or killed someone," I stated. "It looks like they're headed to the east side."

Angel and Real looked at each other with the clandestine knowledge that they were more than likely headed to Maine's.

"Anyway," I said with a dismissive wave of the hand as I tossed my silky black tresses.

"Forget about the police and enough sulking over Kyia not being here. We are going to have the best night ever! We'll just have to do it all over again in South Carolina."

As the limo continued its journey we fell into silence. Each of us was entertaining our own little thoughts while gazing out of the tinted windows at the sights of the city we all loved. There was never a dull moment in this concrete jungle. Something was always happening in the city that never slept. Everywhere that you travel, some form of activity could be observed. The sidewalks were like a never-ending runway where everyday people would strut their stuff, showcasing their own unique styles while sporting some of the hottest names in fashion, from high-end designers to up-and-coming fashionistas. Offering an unending backdrop were buildings that truly scrape the sky with mirrored windows, beveled corners, balconies, marquees advertising the latest and greatest, and rooftop gardens. All of this was spotlighted by a mix of neon and halogen lights that offered an airy glow in colors ranging from soft yellow and amber to bluish green. It was a fascinating tableau for many, and if only for this one night I felt as if the city belonged to me. I was the queen of the night and nothing or no one would ruin it.

In front of the club, admiration skyrocketed at the attire of everyone. People were in their best gear and disembarking from some of the trendiest vehicles. Ladies stepped out in dresses by Prada, Vera Wang, Versace, and Chanel, to name a few. The men would not be outdone, Sporting Ralph Lauren, Marc Jacobs, Tom Ford, and Michael Kors. A casual observer would think a celerity was in attendance because the outside of the club mirrored a red-carpet event. We were giddy with excitement and could hardly wait to shut the club down. As the driver opened the door and offered each of us, in turn, a hand out of the vehicle, all eyes zeroed in, and cameras began to flash from every direction.

Stone had truly gone all out for this event, sparing no expense. He hired professional photographers, and videographers to capture every moment of my special night. I felt like a movie star as we entered the beautifully decorated club. My phone began to vibrate, and I noticed a text message from an unknown number that read,

"I love you and I'm sorry, I have another

surprise for you! I'm coming to see you so don't shoot me! I need to explain, but just in case I'll be wearing my bulletproof jumper suit and a helmet."

"This motherfucker got jokes," I said to myself,

"His sorry ass is trying to test me. He thinks this shit is a game, but I've got something for his ass."

"Everything good?" Angel asked upon seeing her friend's smile turn into a frown.

"Yeah, I'm straight," I said why shaking off the feeling of disgust,

"Just ready to get it poppin."

Angel knew something was wrong, but she brushed it off knowing that pushing the issue would only put her friend on the defensive.

The second level of the club was partitioned into several VIP sections. Once we reached our section, I

BLOOD AIN'T THICKER

thought my eyes were deceiving me until I heard,

> "I wouldn't miss this for the world."
>
> "Kyia!" I screamed embracing her tightly,
>
> "Why didn't you tell me you were coming?"
>
> "It was a surprise. Stone called me and arranged everything. He said your birthday wouldn't be complete if I didn't show up."

Kyia seemed so thrilled to be here. I couldn't help thinking how sweet Stone was. He also knew exactly how to put a smile on my face. Lapsing into the memory of our earlier altercation, my smile became jaded.

> "He's sweet," I acknowledged to myself, "but he's still ain't shit."

All of us gathered for a group hug. Even though Angel and Real were not as close to Kyia as I was, they still had much love for her. We were having a ball, laughing, and acting a fool. A few of my cousins showed up, however, most of them couldn't come. It was time to hit 95 and head south. Lighty was at the bar making his rounds with the ladies, so I made a mental note to inform him of our upcoming trip. The party was awesome, everyone had a great time. Preparing to leave, I thanked the guests for coming, not neglecting to acknowledge everyone who had worked so hard to make my party a success.

"Dessah what's going on?" Angel asked,

"What do you mean we're getting ready to bounce."

"You know exactly what I'm talking about. I didn't see Stone all night. As much as he stays up your ass, for him not to be here at this party, something drastic had to have happened and you're keeping it from me."

"From us." Real joined in as Kyia looked on."

That sorry-ass bastard got a baby on the way, and I told him if he showed up at my party, I was going to put a bullet in his ass. That's what's up are you happy now?" She

BLOOD AIN'T THICKER

screamed.

"Bitch don't go there with me like I'm one of these fake bitches that be smiling in your face but deep down wishing you harm. Hell no, I ain't happy about that shit. I love you like a sister so when you hurt, I hurt. And I knew the moment you walked into Real's house something was wrong. I was concerned about you, not being nosy, and you talk about am I happy now. Bitch, you got me fucked up!" Angel barked as she started to walk away.

Real and Kyia just stared at us. They knew not to interfere and let us handle the minor disagreement independently. This was a pack they made years ago; If one of the four girls had a quarrel with another, they would get it off their chest and no one else will say shit. After the issue was resolved, if necessary, opinions will be accepted by the other girls who were not involved.

This agreement was ineffective if they got into a situation with an outside party. If you had beef with one you had beef with them all. I quickly grabbed Angel's hand to keep her from leaving, knowing that I was dead wrong for lashing out at her like that.

> "I'm sorry, I shouldn't have come at you that way. I was going to tell you about it tomorrow. I didn't want the party ruined."

Looking at my friend through tear-filled eyes,

> "I'm just so hurt. I can't believe he did this to me," I uttered.

> "I know," Angel said while embracing her friend.

> "I'm so sorry he hurt you like this, but you are going to pull through this. Let's get out of here."

Walking towards the waiting limo, I heard someone calling my name. The voice was instantly recognizable. I didn't break stride as I continued walking, totally ignoring Stone.

> "Please, baby, I'm sorry. Just talk to me and

BLOOD AIN'T THICKER

I can explain." Stone pleaded as if his life depended on it.

"Explain? How the fuck can you explain getting another bitch pregnant?" I yelled as his words forced me to acknowledge him.

"Listen, baby, the bitch is lying! Yes, I admit I fucked up. I did have sex with her, but I strapped up every time. This bitch is obsessed. I told her I was not fucking around no more, and then suddenly, the bitch pops up saying she's pregnant. I haven't fucked with her in months. If she was pregnant by me, she would be showing. You saw her did she look pregnant to you?"

I stared him dead in the eyes. It seemed he had been crying or was about to. I wanted to believe him. I loved him so much, but either way, it went, he still cheated and jeopardized our relationship. If it turned out the bitch was lying and I decided to take him back, it was not going to be easy for him.

"You strapped up every time huh? So, this has been an ongoing thing? Go home and continue to enjoy your life because I'm going to enjoy mine." I stated coldly as climbing into the awaiting limo.

Stone stood there feeling utterly defeated. And with no one there to see it, a single tear slid from his left eye, making a trail down his cheek. Watching the love of his life ride away, he hung his head feeling hopeless. He jumped in his car and headed home alone saddened by the day's events. Once I got into the limo I immediately broke down. My crew was hurting from seeing me in so much pain. The four of us rode silently to the Trump Plaza to check into the presidential suite that Stone got me for the weekend.

Finally, Real spoke, "Listen, friend, I know you are hurting right now, and it's a given that Stone fucked up big time. But what if he's telling the truth? He loves you. Shit, even I was about to shed a tear listening to

BLOOD AIN'T THICKER

him begging for forgiveness. Plus, chicks be lying. Hoes will do anything to hold a nigga that's ready to cut them off. You already know fucking with Stone all kinds of bitches are constantly trying to get at him. He is getting money, stay fly, and he's fine as hell. Yeah, he slipped up and fucked a bitch, but you are wifey, and everyone knows that. He loves no one else but you and he shows it. Real concluded with a final nod and fold of her arms."

I sucked my teeth, "Fuck that, I know plenty of niggas out here getting money that hoes stay clocking. If they decide to fuck around, they keep that shit discreet and their wifey never finds out."

"How do you know they never find out? Let me guess… that's what the niggas say, huh? Nine times out of 10, wifey always knows what's going on with her man especially if he is fucking with a chick that knows the game. Most women don't waste time or energy arguing about a side bitch. If the nigga taking care of the home and strapping up, wifey could care less. Especially if you know you're handling your business like a woman is supposed to, why worry? At the end of the day, it gives the wifey a chance to relax both sets of lips. Now, if he starts slacking," Real said with a pregnant pause, "And not handling his responsibilities, then it's time to get in his ass. I know that's not what you want to hear, but I'm just keeping it real with you. If you think another man going to do you better than Stone, remember they all have issues, some greater than others. Nobody is perfect, Dessah. You must weigh the pros and cons. It's sort of like the 80/20 rule."

We immediately began to chuckle thinking of the movie, *Why Did I Get Married?*

"I think you should find out if the bitch is

BLOOD AIN'T THICKER

really pregnant first before you do anything drastic."

"This bastard fertile than a motherfucker, he already got like 10 kids I retorted."

"Stone is a good dude. I hate for us to have to fuck him up!"

The girls erupted into laughter.

"Let's stop all this crying and shit so we can enjoy this fly-ass suite that Stone spent a fortune on for the rest of the weekend," Angel suggested.

Stone Stallion lay restlessly in his king-sized bed thinking about his boo. He was determined to get her back, no matter what. He couldn't understand how he had allowed a woman to get so deep in his heart. Stone had always been labeled a ladies' man and why wouldn't he be? He was 6'2, with brown skin, and soft, curly, dark hair that was always freshly cut. He had beautiful green eyes, a thick West Indian accent, and the cutest dimples. His body was to die for, and his swag was undeniable. He was about his money and always had been, which is why he never got caught up in love until now.

Hydessah was such a lovable person who had drawn him in and had him totally sprung. She started off buying candy from one of his many stores. Then he convinced her to give him some of her candy. Even though she was young, and he had to teach her many things, he had learned so much from her, as well. She was special to him, and he showered her with anything her heart desired. No one will ever be able to fill her shoes. Especially not that trick-ass bitch, Diamond. The thought of her breaking up his happy home made him sit up and forcefully fling a pillar across the room shattering a lamp that stood near the TV. He jumped up and grabbed the dutch off the dresser. Reaching into the top drawer, he pulled out some Arizona and proceeded to roll a blunt, trying to ease his mind.

He picked up his cell phone and checked to see if Dessah had called. As he paced the floor puffing on the blunt, he thought about how he had gotten caught up in the situation. He met Diamond a few months after getting with Dessah. The relationship was so fresh that he felt no loyalty toward her. She was supposed to be just another notch under his belt, like all the rest. Over time things changed, an impenetrable bond developed between her and one of his daughters, and he fell in love. Diamond, on the other hand, was a good fuck who was willing to do anything to please. Dessah had many reservations. There were some things she had never done and was simply not willing to do at the time. During that period, Diamond filled the void. When Stone attempted to end their sexual escapades, she wouldn't back down easily and had an art of seduction that would make any man weak. Occasionally he would give in to the advances, which only made her feel that there was something more between them than just sex. She was determined to fuck her way into a relationship. One day when Dessah popped up at his spot to surprise him, he had just finished receiving some fatal fellatio from Diamond in the backseat of his jeep. He was literally zipping up his pants when he looked out the window before exiting the vehicle and saw Dessah walking toward the front door.

He turned to Diamond and commanded her to stay down in the Jeep until he got his girl in the house, and then to get away from his spot immediately. She sucked her teeth and rolled her eyes with a major attitude, but did exactly as she was told because she knew the deal. When wifey was around no one else mattered.

After coming so close to losing Dessah if he had been caught with the chick in the jeep, he swore to himself that he wasn't fucking around with Diamond again. But he did a few more times, and now he must face the fact that there is a possibility she is pregnant.

He said to himself while reaching for the ashtray, "I've got to prove to my baby that this bitch is lying."

There was no way he would allow that bitch to ruin his future with Dessah.

Kyia chimed as I entered the living room rubbing my eyes. "Good morning, sunshine."

"Good morning. Where is everybody?" I

BLOOD AIN'T THICKER

queried.

"Angel and Real went to pick up y'all's clothes and a few other things. They should be back soon. Are you hungry?"

"Not right now." I said through a yawn.

"I'll get something later."

"Were you able to get any sleep?" Kyia asked my droopy-eyed self. "You're up mighty early."

I sighed, "Not really girl. I couldn't stop thinking about Stone and wondering if he was with that bitch from yesterday."

"Why don't you just call him?"

"And say what? Hello, Stone. I still don't want your sorry ass, but I was checking to make sure you ain't with no other bitch." I said sarcastically.

After hearing me verbalize it Kyia bit her lip and ceded.

"Well, maybe calling him isn't such a good idea right now. But when you calm down you do need to talk to him. Real was right. You need to find out the whole truth before totally letting go of the relationship. You have invested too much time for it to end like this. Plus, it's not going to be as easy as you make it seem with a whole other human involved. That little girl loves you, and you love them both too much to let go."

"I know, I painfully admitted. I just don't want to deal with this right now. I'm going to freshen up. Have one of those ready for me when I get out of the bathroom, I could smell it in the air. Maybe that will help me get my appetite back. You know I love to eat." I said while grabbing my stomach.

Kia laughed good-naturedly. "I got you. Toss me a dutch off the counter over there."

When I left the room Kyia's smile quickly vanished as she thought of her own situation. Giving advice was easy, but she had no clue when it came to dealing with her own problems. They say that problems are just solutions that haven't manifested themselves yet. But her problem was bigger than any solution she could muster in her own strength.

Exiting the bathroom, I stopped at the doorway when I heard Kyia crying while talking on the phone. Whomever she was talking to seemed very upset. The other party could be heard yelling through the phone. Every time Kyia attempted to say anything she was cut off. The person on the other end was controlling the conversation and Kyia's emotions. She was nowhere near being her usual sassy, assertive self. She seemed hurt and afraid.

> "You know it was my girl's birthday, and I told you I will be back in a few days!"

She was finally able to interject.

> "I don't feel like arguing with you about the same shit all the time."

She seemed to be regaining some of her control.

"I'm getting tired of this shit. Since you don't trust me then you need to just leave me alone. And on that note, I'll talk to you later." Kyia said with finality as she hung up the phone and wiped angrily at her tears.

When I heard the end of the conversation, I made my presence known.

"Now I feel much better. Here, you need a light?" I asked her.

"Na," Kyia replied glumly "I got it."

I feigned ignorance and asked, "What's wrong with you? You were so upbeat when I went into the bathroom. What changed in such a short period of time? Are those tears in your eyes? Okay, fess up."

Kyia reluctantly replied, "Girl, it's not that serious. This man is trippin'. He is jealous as a motherfucker. I just get fed up with all the unnecessary arguments."

"Then leave his ass alone." I promptly

BLOOD AIN'T THICKER

advised.

"That's easy for you to say, you cut a nigga off with the quickness. You are the most emotional and emotionless woman I ever met. I love him, and aside from the jealousy he's good to me and loves me."

I pondered and asked an obvious question considering the part of the phone conversation that I overheard.

"Is he abusive?"

Kyia didn't answer right away, then abruptly said, "…No."

I picked up on the delay in responding, "It seems like you hesitated before replying. You wouldn't lie to me, would you?"

Kyia gave a shrug and said, "We've had petty fights; normal things that couples go through. Nothing I can't handle so don't worry about me."

Deep down I knew my friend was dealing with more than she was willing to disclose and decided to do my own investigating to get to the bottom of it.

> "In response to your earlier comment about my emotions, I tend to deal with physical pain way better than I do emotionally. Sometimes I just desire sexual release because I don't have time to feel feelings. My cut-off game is more of a survival mechanism, and if I don't get it in check, I am going to be lonely as hell."

Just as I lit the blunt, Angel and Real walked in.

> "Looks like we're right on time." Real stated, while watching Dessah blow purplish smoke into the air.

> I looked at them and asked, "Where have you two been all morning? And, what's up with the duffel bags?"

Angel and Real smiled at each other with secret knowledge. Angel turned back to me and said,

BLOOD AIN'T THICKER

"Well, we had a few errands to run, and we told you we had a surprise for you."

"Let's see it! You know I'm anxious to find out what it is."

Angel reached into the duffel bag and tossed her a vanilla envelope while singing, "Happy Birthday don't spend it all in one place."

I opened the envelope to reveal 300-hundred-dollar bills neatly stacked with a pink rubber band around it.

"Where did this come from," she asked.

"That's not all," Real replied as she pulled out 14 pounds of Kesha and 5 bricks of coke.

"Damn my day is starting to brighten up already. I'll take the weed you can keep that white girl. Now tell me who the fuck did you hit up."

Angel explained, "When we dropped you

off at Stone's and hit up the liquor store, we ran into an old enemy. You remember what happened to me a few years back?"

I instantly became sad, "How could I forget. That was the worst day of my life."

Mine too Angel said. "Well, I got one of them motherfuckers already and took his stash."

"Why didn't you tell me sooner."

"Because I didn't want to ruin your birthday and then that shit with Stone went down. I didn't even want to tell you now."

As a matter of fact, Real stated, "I killed one of those bastards as well."

Angel looked at her in confusion. "What are you talking about?"

"Do you remember the nigga in the picture with the gray sport coat on, white tee, blue jeans, and gray and white fitted?"

BLOOD AIN'T THICKER

Angel acknowledged with a nod,

> "Well, that was Rick, and I would have never known he was a sick ass rapist. The fucked-up shit is I thought I loved him, but I took care of his ass for you. So, we only got four to go."

Kyia, Angel, and I stood speechless watching Real. We knew how much she cared for Rick. The two of them had been kicking it for a few months, he was all she talked about, and we were finally supposed to meet him at the party.

> "What y'all staring at me all long-faced for, he got what he deserved." She stated coldly.

Angel stared into her friend's eyes and the window to her soul revealed an immense amount of grief. She recognized the overdose of pain in a different form, while hers was physical, Real's was emotional. Trying to look deeper in the window, she blinked and closed the blinds. Something dark had been activated and she feared what it was.

CHAPTER 7

DREAMS & NIGHTMARES

There are two places you can't escape, your dreams and your nightmares. However, if one captures you the other will cease to exist.
(Holli Tabren)

I tapped the turn signal when I spotted the rest stop in Richmond, Virginia. My shift was over, and I was ready to give up the driver's seat to Lighty. In about six more hours we would be in Camden, South Carolina. We went through our normal routine, used the bathroom, got some food, gassed up, and back on the road. Normally, we would get there in 10 hours, but we were riding dirty, so we had to maintain the speed limit.

"Have you given any thought to that other thing?"

Lighty asked.

"Those numbers sound good, but I know nothing about cocaine that's why we got 10 pounds in the car instead of 10 bricks."

BLOOD AIN'T THICKER

"All you need to know is that the money triples up when you get it out of state."

"Okay Rick Ross, talking business using rap verses. Once we touch down and get rid of this weed, I should have a decision. If it's a go I will holler at my Dominican people."

Reclining the seat to a comfortable position, I fell into a deep sleep and felt myself drifting into a dream. The cameras were flashing at all the celebrities entering Club Metrodome in New York City. My cousin had an entertainment company at the time and would throw the most lavish, star-studded, parties in the city. His best friend was an NBA player who always came through with his crew. Although I was only 15 and had no business being in that arena, he figured out a way to get me in. My assigned duties were mailing list and street team for one of the other NBA player's apparel brand. Standing outside the club, my eyes were lasered in on the pink CLK convertible that pulled up to the valet. I witnessed walking art in its truest form exit the vehicle. The woman's show-stopping outfit silenced all the noise and commanded every eye. Her presence was powerful, and I was determined to exude that level of elegance when I entered a room. Aside from her beauty and style, her smile demanded reciprocity. It was infectious and warming. The blaring of a horn scared me out of my sweet dream.

"What happened?" I questioned.

"The car in front of us slammed on its brakes and swerved dodging a deer." Lighty responded.

Thinking about how much I love deer, Bambi popped into my head, and how I cried when they killed his mother. Then suddenly, his daddy decides to pop back into his life when he wasn't there the whole time. Laughing silently at my mental rant, I asked.

"What were they doing in the middle of the highway?"

"The deer are probably saying what is this highway doing in the middle of our forest?" He joked.

BLOOD AIN'T THICKER

Falling back into a deep sleep an uneasy feeling surged through my body and the nightmare began. When the shots rang out, we ran back towards the car. He was on my heels while shooting back at his enemy. I jumped on the driver's side ready to take off, but my protector collapsed before he made it into the vehicle. That's when I noticed the wounds. It only took seconds for his body to be riddled with bullets. My cries were caught in my throat as I cradled his dying, bloody body. Then another nightmare impatiently waiting on the ropes tagged itself in.

Heading towards the sound of a crying baby, I opened the door to what appeared to be a hospital room. Trying to find the baby in distress, I thought my mind was playing tricks on me. The baby was in a jar dead, yet crying out with piercing hazel eyes that penetrated my soul. Walking back towards the door, I slipped and realized I was covered in blood that was gushing out of my womb. It was a horrific sight, and I began to cry out for forgiveness while clutching my belly.

I pleaded with the jar, "Mommy said I was

too young. Please stop crying. I wanted to keep you, but I had no choice."

The body on the concrete and in the clear container turned cold, and so did I.

Waking up dripping in sweat, I felt vengeance and vindictiveness grip each end of my heart to play tug-of-war in slow motion.

I thought to myself, *they caught me slipping, I couldn't protect my protector, or save my promise.* Fervently, I declared never would anyone take my choice. Overanalyzing my declaration, I had to admit that every choice is influenced by something or someone. So, is your choice solely your choice? From that day my choices were influenced by darkness perpetrating as light. Lighty's voice snapped me out of my thoughts.

"We're here," he announced merging off exit 98 on I-20.

We headed to Luch's house, who decided to make South Carolina his home shortly after college. Passing by the barber shop, he established, I laughed thinking about

BLOOD AIN'T THICKER

all the tales that were told during tape-ups. Ironically, I heard more gossip in the barbershop than in the beauty parlor. Luch must have been looking out the window because as soon as we parked the door swung open. And as was the custom when riding dirty, he had a blunt ready to be lit.

In less than two days, 9 pounds were sold, three wholesale, and six broken down. Lighty and I were breaking down the last pound while Black was rolling up when my phone rang. It was my Dominican people, so I stepped out to take the call.

"Do you have some more chronic?" Juan asked.

"I was just breaking down the last one, what's up?"

"My people are here from Atlanta, come through."

Back in the house, Lighty brought up the coke topic again and since the pounds sold so fast, I was all ears.

"It's dry as hell out here, niggas ain't got no money. You know Juan will front you whatever you want." Black added.

Calculating the cost of considering the coke, I never contemplated subtracting integrity, adding deception, dividing loyalty, multiplying betrayal, and receiving a fraction of a century for a sentence.

Turning in the driveway, I noticed the prettiest white paint job on a truck and immediately thought its name must be cocaine. When I entered the house, I laser-locked eyes with the plug's plug. We stared at each other for a few seconds, then he smiled, and I smiled back. Internally I felt self-conscious due to my thugged-out appearance. Being colder than normal in the Carolinas, I had on some fitted jeans, a hoodie, and Timbs with the North Face to match. Standard Harlem attire when handling business. The plug's plug didn't say much, just stared, as he was in the middle of stacking up a duffel bag full of money, while Juan collected the bricks.

Once the transaction was completed and the

BLOOD AIN'T THICKER

money secured, he came into the room where the weed was being distributed. He inquired if I could stay a little longer for him to try the product in case he wanted to buy more before I left. His stare was so intense as if he was reading some type of instruction through my eyes, reluctantly I obliged. Two pulls off the blunt made him decide to purchase everything I had left. Only God could design a human body to be able to have the most intimate conversations with their eyes while simultaneously conversing cordially with their lips. There were no numbers exchanged, promises made, or words spoken. That night I learned a new lens language and all I could see was him.

 The plug's plug watched me pull off through the window and mentally moved me to the top of his radar. He had been watching me for a while and determined that I was as thorough as he had heard. Although it was the first time I met him, it was not the first time he saw me. Still standing at the window, he reflected on that night at Club Cheetahs in NYC.

  L*ooking over my shoulders, I noticed the*

security clearing the way for 14 baddies of all flavors coming into the VIP section. They ordered several bottles, and one of them convinced the bartender to bring them a bowl of fruit which was not a menu option. It was something about her smile and confidence that made my heart skip a beat. I wondered if she always smiled like that and if it mirrored her heart. Watching her interact with friends and random people approaching, I surmised that she was a social butterfly. When one of my homies walked over to greet her, she looked my way briefly but not long enough to lock eyes. So, from that moment I had to figure out a way to know Dessah.

"Why did you have me call Dessah over here when you clearly ain't need no weed?" Juan asked holding up the pound of weed that belonged to the plug's plug.

"Your right, I didn't need any weed, but I wanted her and needed her to see me."

CHAPTER 8

BLOOD AIN'T THICKER

SECRETS & SINS

*Only the dead stay buried; secrets are living tormentors.
Sin is the perversion of a good thing, and eventually, all good things come to an end.
(Holli Tabren)*

Kyia peered out the window of the plane as it was descending on the Charlotte airstrip. She smiled as she thought about how much fun she had hanging out with her girls. If only she could have stayed longer. Aside from the partying she knew her girls needed her because they were dealing with some serious situations, but she had some pressing issues of her own. Plus, if she hadn't gotten back sooner Marcus would have come looking for her. She couldn't understand how in just a few months he had changed from a loving, kind, respectful, confident gentleman to an abusive, controlling manipulative bastard. After being in a relationship for just two years she felt as if she had endured a decade of abuse. But why was she still with him she asked herself. What kind of hold does this man have on me?

As she reflected on her and Dessah's conversation

tears escaped from her eyes. Her friend could see right through her and knew she needed help. How could she tell them about the naïve, depressed, insecure woman she had become? They wouldn't understand what she was going through. She didn't even understand. When the stewardess announced that they could remove their seatbelts she quickly wiped her face while reaching in her purse for her compact. She looked at her reflection in the mirror telling herself that she could handle it and that everything was going to get better. She did this every time that small voice inside was screaming for her to come to her senses, trying to convince herself that she didn't need help. Exiting the terminal, there he was standing in front of his pearl white Porsche Cayenne with a bouquet of flowers flashing his award-winning smile. This was the side of him that won her over and made her heart flutter.

"Hey, baby," he said while placing a passionate kiss on her lips.

"Hey yourself."

"I miss you so much I thought I was going

to have to come on the plane and get you myself."

"Well, here I am so your wait is over."

"That it is baby, that it is."

He quickly placed her luggage in the truck and opened the passenger side door for her to get in.

"Are you hungry," he asked while rubbing his hand up and down her thigh.

"Yes, I could definitely use a bite to eat."

"Good because I cooked your favorite dish plus I have a surprise for you."

"You know I love surprises I can't wait to get home."

On the ride home she told him about her trip and how she enjoyed spending time with her girls. She expressed how much she missed them and told him that they would be coming to visit soon.

"I am so happy you had a great time, and I

can't wait to meet them," he said sincerely.

Pulling into the driveway he reached up and pressed the button on the garage opener. As the garage door rose, Kyia began to scream excitedly and jumped out of the truck.

"Oh my God baby is this for me?"

"Surprise," he said while handing her the keys to her brand-new pearl-white Lexus truck with a big pink bow on it.

"This is so beautiful thank you so much. I love it and I love you."

"I love you too and don't you forget it," he replied in a serious tone, his face hardening for a moment.

"Now come on let's get you cleaned up and fed then you can take it out for a test drive because I have some business to handle later."

She opened the door and could smell the aroma of

BLOOD AIN'T THICKER

barbecue ribs, mac & cheese, corn, potatoes, and collard greens. Her stomach began to growl.

"Your bathwater is waiting on you," he said with a devilish grin.

"I bet it is," she replied as she ascended the stairs.

When she reached the bedroom, he began to undress her in preparation for her bath. She loved how attentive he was, but an eerie feeling came over her and she felt like he was examining her body. She laid back soaking in the tub as she sipped on the glass of wine that awaited her. He watched her intently as he stroked her hair; whispering in her ear how much he loved her and how he would always be there no matter what. After drying her off, he laid her down and began to apply lotion on her body. The warm feeling of his hands instantly hardened her nipples and moisture began to develop between her legs. She let out a soft moan that immediately aroused him. Pulling him on top of her, she stuck her tongue in his mouth. After an hour of lovemaking, they collapsed sweaty and exhausted.

"Now I'm starving," Kyia said still trying to catch her breath.

"Wait right here, I'm going to fix you something to satisfy that hunger."

"Great because my legs don't work at all."

Kyia started to feel a sense of hope as she thought about the direction her relationship was heading. She knew if she remained faithful and prayed hard enough Marcus would turn back into the man she initially fell in love with.

"Dinner is served," he said while placing her tray in front of her.

While she was eating her food, he took a quick shower and got dressed.

"Where are you going?"

"I told you earlier, I have some business to handle. I will be back soon keep the bed warm for me."

Kyia woke up at three in the morning to a faint

buzzing sound coming from her pocketbook. She looked over for Marcus noticing that his side of the bed was empty again. There were several missed calls on her phone, one from Marcus and a few from an unknown number. Before she was able to check her messages a video text popped up. When she opened it, her heart sank. Marcus was in a 69 position with some light skin bitch. She couldn't stand to continue watching the sexual escapades that seemed to last 23 minutes. At least that is how long the video was. Along with the video was a text that read,

> "Stay away from my husband bitch he will never leave me."

Kyia sat back on the bed and cried her eyes out. She was so mad at herself for allowing this to happen and so tired of forgiving his indiscretions. Tired of all his lies and excuses so she forwarded the video to his phone. Kyia wondered how long it would take for him to come home and what he could possibly say to explain this one. Why did love have to hurt so bad? She was willing to do anything to please him and fulfill all his needs.

"Why did he do this to me? Why do I keep letting him hurt me so badly? What is wrong with me? There is no way he could fix this. I am fed up, this motherfucker has got to go," she screamed as she pulled all his clothes out of the closet and threw them over the stairs.

After tiring herself out from tossing clothes and shoes, she made a drink, lit a blunt, and cried some more not knowing what else to do. Realizing that none of it helped her heart, she decided to call on God and asked him to help her get through this. She felt like a hypocrite coming to him knowing she was living in sin and had been for many years. She wasn't ready to let go of a lot of things, but she always found comfort in prayer. This time was different though she still felt the heavy burden after talking to God.

"Maybe He is tired of listening to me," she told herself.

After drinking a bottle of Hennessy and smoking two blunts, she decided to take a shower hoping the warm water would calm her body giving her a relaxing feeling. Exiting the shower, she decided to put his clothes in a neat little pile near the door. No need to destroy her house knowing she would have to clean it up. She changed the sheets they had made love on the day before and fluffed her pillows. By that time her eyes were so heavy she decided to lie down and get some sleep.

Marcus sat outside his stash house with his man Chance. He had not been home in three days. Knowing he fucked up for the thousandth time he contemplated what he could possibly do or say to get out of this situation. Showing Chance, the video text that Kyia forwarded, he cursed himself. Thinking with his little head caused him to hurt Kyia yet again. Breaking her heart was the last thing he wanted to do but he simply was not a one-woman man. He knew he was being selfish but that's just how he lived his life. She would eventually forgive him like she always did. He just needed to give her some time. He knew Kyia was the realest woman he ever met. She loved him with all her heart, but he didn't know how to love her the same way, so he loved her the only way he knew how. By providing all her needs and giving her everything she wanted except loyalty. He felt like as long as she was taken care of, she should not worry about what he did in the streets. She had his heart, and nobody could take that away no matter how well they performed sexually.

> "Damn homie, how did you let that girl get to your phone?" Chance asked.
>
> "Man, I fucked up that bitch is slick as hell. I beat her ass for that shit though."
>
> "You know Kyia ain't going nowhere, but you have some serious making-up to do."
>
> "I done bought her everything under the sun the last six times I got caught up."
>
> "Six times nigga, do you even try to do shit on the low or you just don't give a fuck?"
>
> "Ain't that, bitches come and go. I love her and all, but I have loved before, so I can love again if it comes to that. The only thing I truly love is money and if I have that I can

have any bitch I want. So, if she decides she no longer wants to ride with me, I'll just give somebody else the seat, simple as that."

"You cold as hell."

Rick's death triggered the nightmares, and they came back with a vengeance.

"Mommy please help me; I need you Mommy he's hurting me make him stop. Please mommy I can't get him off me he's too strong."

Empyreal jumped up frantically relieved to have escaped another terrifying nightmare. They seemed to come back more frequently ever since that night at Rick's. She grabbed her pillow and pulled it close to her chest trying to suppress the anger that was building up in her body. It had been years since she had been raped and brutalized by one of her mother's many boyfriends. Even though the physical abuse ended the emotional scars were still present. She got up and made herself a cup of tea hoping to calm her nerves, wondering why her life had to be full of so much pain and deception.

The woman who birthed her and was supposed to love her allowed men to sexually abuse her. Real thought her mother Darla, was the most beautiful woman in the world. Having never met her father her mother was all she had. Once she turned nine years old it seemed as though the love her mother had for her turned into hate. She felt like Real had taken her life away and she was stuck raising a child that no man wanted to be a daddy too. Darla always had a sick and twisted way of thinking. She was a man-pleaser and no matter what, she was willing to do anything to keep one even if it meant sacrificing her own daughter.

Darla's cycle of sexual abuse began long before she was born, her mother went through it, grandmother, and great-grandmother. It was a generational curse that ended with her. She would never harm her child or allow anyone to. Why couldn't her mother be strong enough to protect her? She reasoned that her strength and personality came from her father's side. Even though her mother allowed her to go through years of torture, Real

BLOOD AIN'T THICKER

still regretted taking the life of the woman who gave her life. But she had no remorse for killing her perverted boyfriend, David.

When Real turned 14 she felt as though she was going to go crazy if she didn't stop the abuse. At this point, her mother began to physically abuse her while David sexually abused her. She felt like a sex slave and a punching bag wrapped in one. Tonight was going to be the last time either one of them was going to put a hand on her ever again. She had it all planned out after borrowing a gun from one of the corner hustlers' stash. She had been learning how to shoot on the project rooftops since she was 10. She knew David and her mother would be going out for David's birthday that night, so she waited in the dark alley two blocks from her house knowing the route they often took after leaving the local bar. Around 4:00 am they came stumbling toward Real and she was cocked and ready. Happy birthday David she said as she put one bullet between his legs and the other between his eyes. Darla didn't have a chance to scream as the same fate awaited her. She removed their wallets and jewelry before exiting the alley. After wiping the gun down, Real returned it to the hustler's stash. She hurried home got rid of the oversized clothes she wore and went to bed. She prayed that God would forgive her, oblivious to the eyes lurking in the city that never sleeps. The alarm clock snapped her out of her thoughts.

Pulling into the parking lot Angel checked her rearview mirror making sure she wasn't being followed. She surveyed the array of cars parked outside seeing if she recognized any of them. Having developed a feeling of paranoia combined with embarrassment caused her to sit in the car for another 20 minutes before exiting. She knew Muyana would be impatiently waiting on her at the bar. There was a war going on inside her soul. The battle between her heart and her mind was creating a whole lot of stress in her life. She worried how her girls would feel about her alternative lifestyle. Hiding her emotions and desires for other women was becoming a burden. After all she'd been through, they would have to understand that the thought of a man touching her sexually made her skin crawl.

Women on the other hand were different. They understood her, their touch was gentle, and their skin was always so soft. Penetration was something she never wanted to feel again. Then there was Muyana the most beautiful woman she had ever seen. The half-black half Brazilian combination coupled with a sexy shortcut and dynamic body was who had her on an emotional high. She hated the fact that their relationship had to be on the down low until she had enough courage to tell her family. Some days she woke up with that I don't give a fuck attitude. The thought of hurting the people she loves the most breaks her heart. She really worried about Auntie Julia taking it the hardest, but this was her life, and she was going to live it the way she wanted.

> "Hey, what took you so long I thought you got lost," Muyana said in her thick Brazilian accent while kissing her softly on the lips.
>
> "Sorry about that baby I had a very important phone call that I had to finish."

"It's Okay, I ordered you a drink come on let's go dance."

Angel followed behind her as she switched her way to the dance floor. Just watching her walk turned Angel on. She was ready to call it a night but knew how important it was for them to spend time together outside of the bedroom. So, she put her hormones in check, and they danced the night away.

Angel woke up still feeling a little hung over from the night before. Her vision was a little blurry as she tried to adjust her eyes to the bright light shining in from the blinds. Getting out of bed, she felt Muyana pulling her back down.

> "I have to go check on one of my shops," she whispered. "I will see you later, I promise."

> Muyana sat up straight pouting. "Can I at least fix you some breakfast before you go?"

Angel looked at her watch realizing she was already getting a late start.

BLOOD AIN'T THICKER

"I would love to, but I can't. Don't give me that look you know I hate when you start pouting. I promise I will make it up to you later."

She figured since she was in the Bronx, she would stop by her shop on Fordham Road. It had only been two months since she opened, and it stayed packed. Angel knew that going into business with Maria was a power move. She had a huge clientele and her whole staff worked hard. Since she was brutalized and left for dead many years ago money was her motivation, and she was driven by revenge. The closer she got to her enemies the easier it would be for her to destroy them. If information needed to be found, its location would be the beauty shop.

Angel inhaled the sweet scent of the strawberry poundcake wallflower that tantalized her senses when she entered the shop. While flipping on the switches, she was startled by the blaring volume of the television. Grabbing the remote to turn it down, she noticed a familiar face plastered across the screen and listened intently as the journalist reported,

> "Frank Franco, a known drug dealer was found brutally murdered in his apartment."

Angel got all queasy inside and a smile spread across her face as she reflected on how good it felt to kill Maine. Now another face from the photo of dead men that hung on his wall was eliminated and it turned her on. She was on the verge of exploding at the thought of killing Tyrone next when the ringing of her phone snapped her out of her fantasy.

> Once she hit that green button, she went in, "You sure know how to call somebody right back."
>
> I chuckled before responding, "My apologies, I just got back in town and have been contemplating moving to South Carolina for a while."
>
> "I ain't trying to hear none of that blasphemy. What's a city girl like you going to do in the country? My day started off

lovely and here you go talking crazy. Anyway, we will discuss this later I have to make a call."

Angel ended the call and felt as if a piece of her heart chipped off. She reasoned that I was just on one of my purpose-driven journeys again and would eventually realize my compass was broken because South Carolina was in the wrong direction. Dismissing the thought of losing her friend to forest living, she decided to call her Auntie Julia. Ever since she moved out almost a year ago, they hadn't seen that much of each other. The phone rang for the fourth time before she answered. It seemed like she was out of breath.

"Hey Auntie, did I interrupt something?"

"Hey baby girl you know nothing else matters when you call."

Even if I was in the middle of a climax, she thought to herself, but wouldn't dare say on the phone.

"Where are you baby? I miss you."

"I am running some errands right now, but I

was thinking maybe we could get together for an early dinner."

Rushing her off the phone, Julia said, "Sounds great, just call me when you are on your way to pick me up. Love you, bye."

When Angel heard the dial tone, she looked at the phone and laughed to herself.

Julia couldn't wait to get her niece off the phone so she could get back to business. She would have never let her interrupt the climax that she was so close to reaching, but the last thing she wanted was for Angel to stop by, let herself in and catch her with both legs in the air. After going through so much with her in the past few years she thought it was best not to bring any men into the house. So, her personal life was completely separated. Now that Angel moved out of the house, she was more comfortable having her rendezvous in her own home.

Even though she missed Angel living with her, she enjoyed how good it felt to make love in her own bed.

BLOOD AIN'T THICKER

After reaching her fifth orgasm she was drained and just wanted to cuddle up and fall asleep. Unfortunately, she would be doing that alone. Her lover had to get back home to his wife. He was supposed to be going to pick up something for the house and has been gone all morning. When he got up to take a shower she simply asked when she would see him again knowing it was no use protesting him leaving so soon. She realized how complicated his situation was and no matter how great their sexual chemistry was he would never leave his wife.

> "Don't worry baby we will get together again real soon. You know I can't stay away from you too long; I am planning a weekend getaway for us in a couple of months."

He dried off, got dressed, and kissed her goodbye. She got out of bed feeling like a fool. This was how she always felt when he left her. Full of mixed emotions, her mind was telling her what she was doing was wrong, but her body was always yearning for his touch. He met her every need, except for time. She reasoned that at her age all the men that were worth being in a relationship with were married. Plus, she knew plenty of women who were happy mistresses. She figured, what he was giving her was better than being alone. Her conscience was eating away at her, but she continued to justify her actions. *You are a homewrecker, deceiver, slut, disloyal, and a untrustworthy woman* is what her mind reprimanded, but she had fallen in love with a married man and was not willing to let him go. She took a nice warm bath and decided to take a nap until it was time to get dressed for dinner.

CHAPTER 9
MURDER-CYCLE

If the gun could talk, the bullets would tell a tale of toil: tearing through flesh while ripping families apart. (Holli Tabren)

Trina sat in her living room shuffling through the multiple bags she had scattered on the floor.

"Frankie, come here baby mommy has a surprise for you."

Separating all the things that she purchased for him made her heart smile. He was such a good boy who was extremely smart and stayed on the honor roll in school. Frankie knew his mother struggled to provide for him since his dad was never around. So, he never asked for much but appreciated everything.

One afternoon while Trina was helping Frankie with his homework, he looked up at her with his big bright eyes and said,

"Mom, if you get some extra money can you buy me a PlayStation? All the kids at school are talking about it and I can watch DVDs on it too since our DVD player is broken."

"I tell you what, you continue to keep those grades up and I will work really hard to get you that game system."

"Thanks, mom you're the best."

Frankie gave his mother the biggest hug and kiss then turned his attention back to his homework. Trina stared at her son for a while trying to figure out how she would come up with the money to buy something so expensive. She left her son at the table and went into the bathroom to call his father.

"Hello, Frank it's Trina are you busy?"

"I stay busy what's good," he replied.

"Well, I was wondering if you would help me buy a PlayStation for Frankie. He's doing well in school; he doesn't get in trouble, and he never asks for anything. So, I know this will mean a lot to him."

"Look Trina I'm not trying to hear all that shit I ain't got no money."

"What the fuck you mean you ain't got no money. You hustle all fucking day. I have been struggling to take care of our son by myself for nine years and I never asked you for shit."

"Look bitch, I ain't got no money for you or that kid. Now, if you want some dick holler at me, I may have a couple of dollars then otherwise don't call me."

Trina sat at her bed in tears she couldn't believe she had such a wonderful son by such a fucked-up nigga. *That motherfucker is going to get his one day,* she said to herself. Wiping the tears from her eyes, Frankie walked into the room.

"Mommy, I'm finished," he said with excitement.

As he handed over the homework for his mother to

review, he noticed her face.

> "Mommy, why are you crying? If you can't get the game system, it's okay; I don't want you to be sad."

> "No baby it's not that. I'm fine someone made me upset on the phone, but everything is all right."

> "It was Frank, wasn't it?"

> "What did I tell you about that," his mother scolded.

> "Why do I have to call him Dad? He doesn't act like one, he's never here, he does nothing for me, and he always makes you cry."

> "Listen, don't worry about the problems your father and I go through. You are his son, and he loves you even if you think he doesn't."

> "How can you tell me not to worry mom? What he does to you affects me. I hate to see

BLOOD AIN'T THICKER

> you struggling all the time pretending to be happy in front of me. I hear you crying late at night, and I cry too but when I grow up you won't have to struggle anymore, I am going to take care of you."

Trina was astonished by the way her son was talking to her. She knew he was not being disrespectful but was speaking from his heart.

> "Frankie, I understand how you feel and even though it is hard I want you to focus on enjoying childhood. I don't want you to grow up too fast. Being an adult is challenging and requires you to take on a lot of responsibilities. Though we struggle some days, always remember tough days don't last but tough people do. Your mommy is extremely tough especially when she cries at times. Now, you can go outside with your friends for a while until dinner gets ready."

> "Okay, I love you,"

"And I love you more," Trina said while giving him a forehead kiss.

As she headed to the kitchen her cell phone rang.

"Trina speaking."

"Hey Trina, have you seen Frank?" Ty asked.

"No, but I just got off the phone with his sorry ass."

Oh really, well he has been ducking me for weeks. I got a proposition for you."

After reflecting on the events that led up to her agreeing to set up her son's father, she started to feel overwhelmed with guilt. Even though she hated him now she did love him at one time. She knew if Ty was out to get him eventually, he would be found. So regardless of the role she played he would be dead anyway. She tried to convince herself that she really had no choice but to comply. Plus $10,000 was more money than Frank gave her throughout the whole relationship. His death constantly weighed heavy on her heart. However, she felt

BLOOD AIN'T THICKER

better knowing Frank could not be a father to her son rather than he just wouldn't. *Fuck it,* she said to herself, *Frankie would not miss something he never had, which was a relationship with his father.*

"Frankie, I know you heard me call you the first time."

Running down the hall out of breath, Frankie said, "Mom, I'm coming I was just trying to finish up my set."

"Set? What are you talking about?"

"I was working out and I was in the middle of my push-ups. I must do 10 sets of 10."

"Oh yeah, where did you learn that?"

"I have been watching this personal trainer on TV, he's really cool. Some of the stuff is too hard for me to do right now but the push-ups and sit-ups will help me build muscle so I can be ready to try out for football next year."

HOLLI TABREN

"Okay, come see what I have for you."

When Frankie pulled the PlayStation out of the bag his face lit up, he was the happiest kid in the world.

"Oh, mom this is the best present ever."

Once he retrieved everything from the bags he had five new games, four pairs of sneakers, tons of clothes, and a laptop with educational apps programmed in it. He was so excited he didn't know which game he wanted to play first.

"Mom, can Emmy come over and play with me for a little while please?"

"If his mother agrees then it is fine with me."

"Before you come back go to the store and get some milk for the mac and cheese."

Wow, mom, you have really outdone yourself. New clothes, games, and my favorite meal, this is great."

Playfully punching Frankie on the arm,

BLOOD AIN'T THICKER

Trina said. "Boy if you don't go ahead with your grown self, I see those push-ups working already, arms feeling like bricks."

Preparing dinner, she heard a noise at the front door, and she almost dropped the pot on her foot. *I know that boy ain't back that fast, he probably forgot something,* she said to herself. She proceeded to the front door to see why he was turning at the doorknob. Maybe he forgot his keys,

"I'm coming boy," she yelled.

When she made it to the door, she heard a loud bang, and before she knew it her door was kicked open. She looked up and saw Breeze and Drew rushing towards her, guns drawn. Terror instantly invaded her body and all she thought about was her son. Lord, please don't let them hurt my baby she silently prayed to herself as she took off running down the hall. Breeze was on her heels and quickly snatched her by the hair dragging her back toward the living room. Trina tried to fight to get out of Breeze's grips to no avail. She cried and screamed asking why they were doing this to her. Drew swiftly lifted her to her feet and placed his hand around her neck nearly cutting off her air supply.

"Shut up bitch and I will make this as painless as possible."

She pleaded, "Wait please I have a son don't do this."

"That is right, Breeze go check the house and see if that little nigga is in here so he can join his mother."

"No please he's just a baby and he's not here anyway."

"Well for his sake let's hope he's not," Drew stated coldly.

Everything's clear, now let's get this over with and get out of here," Breeze said.

Trina knew her life was about to be over, but before it ended, she asked God for forgiveness and prayed that her son would not be punished due to her sins. *Please take care of my baby he's such a good boy*

BLOOD AIN'T THICKER

she kept repeating to herself.

"What is she saying?" Drew asked.

"I think she is praying. Too late bitch, God can't help you now, Breeze sadistically stated."

Positioning the barrel of the 45 in the middle of her forehead, he pulled the trigger. Her lifeless body fell to the floor. Screams from the doorway caused the two men to turn around and face the two young boys watching them. Frankie dropped the milk he purchased for his mom and was staring at the two men that just took her life right before his eyes. He was so scared, but he told himself to run as the men were headed toward them. In no time he took off running. As he ran out the front door of the building, he heard two shots but didn't turn around he thought they were shooting at him, so he kept running. He began to cry as visions of his mother's body hitting the floor replayed in his mind. He was so filled with fear and grief that he paid no attention to where he was running. Out of nowhere the sound of screeching tires caused him to pause and instantly everything went black.

HOLLI TABREN

"Somebody help me please oh my God please be okay. Please somebody call an ambulance, please.

Destiny stood over the little boy who ran in front of her car crying hysterically praying that he wasn't dead. Little Frankie laid in the middle of the street motionless surrounded by pedestrians crying and praying. Paramedics hurried over to the little boy and placed him on the gurney, rushing him to the hospital. As Frankie was taken away in the ambulance Destiny leaned on her car crying and in shock. As the police approached to question her, screams could be heard from a woman across the street.

"They killed my Emmy, oh my God, they took my baby from me she wailed."

"Ma'am, please stay right here" the officer said as he ran towards the screaming woman to see what was going on.

Getting closer to the woman, his knees began to buckle as he watched a mother cradling her little boy covered in blood. Immediately, he called for backup.

> Looking into the cop's eyes, she tearfully said. "They killed my baby! Why did they kill my Emmy?"

Stone hadn't seen Dessah in six months and even though he had indulged in several different women since then trying to get her out of his system he missed her dearly. Even though Diamond was lying about carrying his seed she succeeded in ruining his relationship. No matter how hard he tried to express to Dessah how sorry he was and how much he needed her she was not giving him another chance. She acted as if she never loved him at all. He knew he hurt her deeply and figured if he gave her some time, she would eventually come around but that hasn't happened yet. He needed to see her, touch her, feel her again. His heart felt hollow, and she was the only woman who could fill it up. His thoughts were interrupted by the ringing of his phone.

> "What's good Homie you ready?" His partner asked as the loud music was blaring

through the phone.

"Walking out the door right now, meet me at the spot, Stone responded."

Snatching his fitted cap off the dresser, he drove towards his spot. His mind was racing but it was time to handle business. He had to get Dessah out of his system, so he could focus on the situation at hand. His business had just started to pick back up to normal within the last few months. Prior to that, the police made it hard to make money while they were investigating Maine's murder. After so many dead-end leads the case went cold and business heated up. Now he and his crew faced another dilemma. The Brooklyn niggas was trying to infiltrate his territory by selling the same product not adhering to the original agreement that was made when Maine was still alive. So, it was time to prepare his team for war. There was no way these fake ass gangsters were going to blatantly disrespect him like this. When he pulled up to the spot, he parked and sat in the car momentarily. Looking at his whole squad posted up, they were ready for whatever. He wondered if they were truly ready for what was about to go down. His crew had heart, but it took more than that to win this battle. He knew there would be casualties. Was he prepared for all the blood that would be on his hands? Or all the fatherless children that he would have to help take care of? What if innocent people got caught up could he sleep at night knowing he set everything in motion? He took another puff off the blunt before tossing it out of the window along with the what-ifs. This was the life he chose to live and there were different rules in these streets. Decisions had to be made some tougher than others. The things that we hate the most are necessary to survive in this game.

> "Dammit, I thought you were never going to get out of the car," his little man yelled out of the crowd.

Before Stone could reply with something slick the sound of screeching tires could be heard and within seconds shots rang out. He immediately pulled his Glock from his waist and started letting off. The war had begun.

CHAPTER 10
CHOICES & CONSEQUENCES

If you ever forget the effect of your choices, consequences will always help you remember.

(Holli Tabren)

Ty headed toward the hospital room that he had been visiting for the past five years. Every time he looked at his big brother who was in a coma, he reflected on that night he got the phone call. He had just left the club before it got too crazy trying to exit plus, he had some business to handle in the early a.m. As soon as he got on the FDR his phone started blowing up.

"Ty, I'm sorry it happened so fast," his brother's right-hand man screamed through the phone.

"What are you talking about? Where is my brother?

"They took him to the hospital."

BLOOD AIN'T THICKER

Ty began making numerous calls to find out all the details of the incident. After talking to the person with answers he was informed that his brother was hit in the head with a bottle by the same chick he was kicking it with in VIP. He vowed that night to make that bitch pay.

Every visit he believed that his brother would wake up. Walking down the hospital hall, he thought his eyes were deceiving him. His elementary school crush was sitting outside a hospital room in tears. When he approached her, his heart fluttered. She looked up and knew exactly who he was and held him tightly apologizing for her appearance as she too was crushing on him.

"Who you here to see?" He asked.

"This little boy that I hit by accident. I have been here every day waiting on him to wake up. No one else has come to visit, I think he is a runaway and I just want to help him."

Ty didn't know it then, but this connection was compounded with complexities.

HOLLI TABREN

Empyreal grabbed her keys off the ottoman and headed out the door. Before she cranked the car her phone rang. Since she didn't recognize the number, the caller was sent straight to voicemail. Once her voicemail notification sounded, she was curious to know who this unknown caller was. Listening to the message made her instantly regret pressing play.

> "Empyreal Harris this is Sally Salters calling from the coroner's office. We have been desperately trying to reach you for the past month regarding your sister Trina Harris. Please contact our office as soon as possible. You will also need to contact social services regarding your nephew Frankie Harris who is currently hospitalized in a coma."

Empyreal grabbed her chest, closed her eyes and reminisced on the last time she saw her sister's face. It had been nearly ten years ago when their mother Darla kicked Trina out for getting pregnant. She was crying and begging Darla to let her stay, pleading that she had nowhere to go. But Darla was a cold-hearted bitch, and all the crying fell on deaf ears. Real tried to hold on to her sister as tight as she could, but her arms weren't strong enough, so Darla ripped her away, along with a piece of her heart. Staring through the saddest, teary eyes, Trina told her baby sister how much she loved her and that she would come back for her, but she never did. Real felt her cycle of pain progressing and it was about to be unleashed.

Rykyia Graham, the doctor will see you now. It had been nearly a month since she heard from Marcus and had not been feeling well lately. So, she decided to get a full physical to see what was going on in her body. Greeting the doctor upon his entry into the room, she got so nervous. After reviewing her chart, he informed her that all her tests came back negative except for one. In eight months, she was going to be a mother. Kyia didn't know how to feel or respond so she thanked the doctor for his assistance and ran to her car where she broke down. *Now what am I going to do, she thought to herself.* When she dialed Marcus' number a woman answered whose voice sounded oddly familiar, so she hung up and cried harder pulling at her belly.

Angel locked up the shop preparing to meet Julia for their dinner date. She made a mental note to stop by the flower shop to purchase an arrangement for her. After selecting the perfect bouquet, she reached for a teddy bear and a paralyzing feeling overshadowed her. Instinctively, she grabbed at her waist before turning around, but her gun was left in the car. Although she felt a threat, there was none in sight. No one else was in the store, but she knew an enemy was close. Her heart started racing, she grabbed at her chest and walked out of the store to prevent a panic attack. The streets were so busy she didn't know which way to look, yet her brain continued to send her body warning signals. The hospital entrance demanded her attention and that's when she saw a man and a woman exiting. *This can't be happening, that can't be him,* she said to herself.

CHAPTER 11
THE PLUG'S PLUG

The power of the electricity that will surge through you, is contingent on the source you are connected to.
(Holli Tabren)

After several trips up and down Interstate 95, I decided to settle in the South. Starting off in an apartment complex, I paid the rent for six months to give me time to stack. Then transitioned to my first house with goals of living there for a year and applying to a local college where I wouldn't pay an in-state fee. Admittedly, I was trying to redeem myself for blowing $27,000 of my daddy's money on one semester at the University of Maryland. It wasn't the academia that was an issue, I just didn't show up because I was too busy slinging pounds. My mother teased me every chance she got by sporting the college logo hoodie declaring they paid $27,000 for a sweatshirt.

Opening the blinds I noticed the cocaine-colored truck pulling into the driveway. Over the past few visits,

I had gotten to know the plug's plug and was able to fulfill my cousins' requests by connecting them to the source. Maintaining my relationship with my baby girl was something the plugs plug couldn't digest. She was another man's child that I did not birth, and he couldn't understand our bond. Well, the feelings were mutual when it came to Briangela, because she felt like he took her daddy's place, and his daughter was taking hers. I saw baby girl every time I went to New York and brought her to the south in the summers. On her last trip, we all went to Great Wolf Lodge in West Virginia. It was an emotional disaster for Briangela, and she never came back. It broke my heart that I couldn't get him to understand that I had enough love for them all.

Within a month of dating the plug's plug, he began to upgrade everything. Bigger more lavish jewels, a restaurant business, a newer car, a bigger house, and bought my first Real Estate book. At first, I was enraptured with how much he adored me, but then his protection turned possessive. For every item he added, he expected a piece of my independence as a return. Have

BLOOD AIN'T THICKER

you ever felt you had everything and nothing at the same time? His mama told me stories of how his daddy would kidnap her, locking her in the house for days to be certain of her whereabouts. The plug's plug was definitely like his daddy.

One night he went insane about my ringtone, and I felt he must be guilty about something because his energy was way off. Throughout our relationship, I never had a female approach me or ring my line about any indiscretions. Denial never being a part of my vocabulary, I was sure he had a few, but the dudes with the long money seem to be able to keep their side chicks in check. It is the short-money niggas that have chicks calling your phone and running up to you talking about they are pregnant. That night I took a shower and prayed that God would get me out of this toxic situation. *Be careful what you pray for.*

A few hours prior to shutting down the restaurant, Black hit me up to remind me about the party at Plums. Then he added that his man from high school called for some work that he was low on. So, Lighty snatched up what he needed while I paid and prepared my employees for the next day.

When we pulled up to the block, Black informed us that his man changed the location of the meeting, and needed a ride. So, he hopped in the back of my truck and instantly I felt as if I had to use the bathroom. Deciding to hold it since we were going to our aunt's house afterward to get dressed, we proceeded to the destination. That decision would ultimately take me on a life-changing detour. We pulled up to the meeting spot and Black's man jumped in the back. He made small talk with both Black and Lighty as they all went to school together. I said nothing because I had never seen him before. However, my ears perked up when he said,

"I got to get the money out of the car."

That eerie feeling surged through my body again. Something was wrong and before I knew it police were everywhere. They say the most important part of any plan is the getaway, but who plans on your cousin's high school friend setting him up? I had about three grand in my purse and an ounce of weed that I was smoking. The detective searching through my purse asked where I got the weed from. My response was,

"That's irrelevant."

He told me I would be begging to talk to him within 72 hours. He's still waiting on that call. Seventy-two hours and one second later, my hold was lifted, and I bonded out. Once I got in the car my brother took me to the plug's plug who was waiting at a restaurant knowing I would be hungry. He was sitting at the bar when I walked in. Making my way toward him, he began speaking lens language. He told me he hadn't slept in days, and that if I would have just used the Real Estate book he bought me, I wouldn't be in this mess. The closer I got, the cloudier his lens became. He was one of the most emotional gangsters I knew. No matter how much my bond was, he was coming to my rescue. Once in arms distance, he embraced me tighter than he ever had before. Even though he didn't love me the way I thought he should, he loved me the only way he knew how and that was with everything he had.

HOLLI TABREN

For two years and 10 months, I was out on bond, while the state's key witness recovered from the nine shots he survived. I went to Real Estate School and got my license. Century 21 Bob Capes was where I started, and it was eventually acquired by Coldwell Banker United. It took me eight months to sell my first home, then I sold three within the same month. That year I was $40,000 shy of being titled a millionaire agent. For clarity, not a million in profit just sales. Realizing that the same skills used in the streets can be applied in the boardroom, I walked in my element. Granted the money was not as fast as moving bricks, but brick by brick something solid could be built on a firm foundation.

In the Real Estate merger, the individual offices became shared spaces and my office bunky would eventually become my bestie. We were total opposites and had nothing in common, but she was everything I needed for the journey I would soon embark on. Knox was a Bible-toting, Testament gum chewing, Scripture mint eating, part-time Christian bookstore job having, woman on fire for the Lord. I didn't know it then, but

BLOOD AIN'T THICKER

Knox was the radical faith I needed. For my birthday, she bought me a Joyce Meyers amplified Bible, which broke down each verse of scripture enabling me to understand them. The more I read, the more questions I had, and she was ready and willing to answer. Unbeknownst to either of us, Knox was planting a seed of promise.

Almost 2 years into my Real Estate career, my lawyer informed me that jury selection was underway. That morning I woke up to the smell of home fries and other goodies, mama was cooking. She came down south to help me set up the restaurant due to her experience in food service. When I got arrested, I begged her not to tell my dad because it would tear his heart apart. I was his Pumpkin, his Diddleboops, and no matter how old I got he continued to call me those pet names.

Entering the kitchen, Mom asked,

"When are you going to tell your father?"

I was trying to hold off in case I never had to tell him due to the case being thrown out or probation granted. My mom looked at me deeply and I saw the tournament in her eyes when she said,

> "You are going away for a while, God told me."

> "What mama? I need you to be more optimistic about this."

> "Sorry baby, but my dream last night confirmed what my heart was trying to prepare me for. I felt this pain in my womb and it reminded me of the same pain you gave me when you were in my belly. Then suddenly you were ripped away from me and I knew what that meant. Don't worry baby, I'm going to come to visit you in your orange jumpsuit."

My appetite was ruined, and I understood the assignment, it was time to write my daddy that letter.

CHAPTER 12

VISION

You don't need to see to have vision, but you need vision to see. (Holli Tabren)

When the judge rendered the verdict and delivered the sentence, my heart shattered.

"You are hereby sentenced to the South Carolina Department of Corrections for a mandatory period of 25 years."

It felt as if something escaped my body. Was it my soul? Was it all the dreams and visions I had for my life? Not sure, but I felt barren. My first thought was of never being able to experience motherhood aside from being a bonus mom. This concern of conceiving was the most challenging part of the consequence. Then I looked at my mother standing there pleading with the judge for mercy. All the pain and turmoil that I caused her over the years was etched on her tear-covered face. Looking into the judge's eyes, I saw a hint of compassion as he responded,

"Sorry ma'am there's nothing I can do."

He was right I blew a trial and something in my spirit told me that the only One who could Judge my case and change my conviction was the Man who made man, that was more than just a Man. Seeing my mother standing there looking defeated turned the fragmented pieces of my heart into dust and all I could say was,

"I'm sorry."

As I was escorted away in handcuffs I wondered if she believed me. Countless I'm sorry had begun to fall on deaf ears, but I truly meant it this time. *Or did I?* The consequences of the choices I made with the chances I'd been given were insurmountable. Along my ride to the processing center to prepare for prison, I felt my heart slowly rebuilding its construction. Admittedly, prior to its fortification, bitterness, anger, betrayal, vengeance, and worthlessness penetrated through and claimed its dwelling place. It amazes me how when life deals us the hand we shuffled, we want to blame others for losing the game. It's inevitable that the seemingly reliable deck that was once firm and solid soon became faded, flexible, and began sticking together. Although my cousins conspired

BLOOD AIN'T THICKER

together, betrayed me, and violated the laws of the streets, my blindness coupled with my lack of vision ultimately destroyed me. *Should I have cut the deck? Is it too late to throw away the old cards and start over with a fresh deck?*

Mail call was one of the most anticipated times of the day, second to visitation. Today I received the realest letter I would ever receive throughout my entire sentence. It read,

"Listen, don't depend on nobody to keep their promises. People are going to disappoint you, get used to it, even me. Understand, while you're in there doing time life is still happening and everyone deals with life differently. So don't think people don't love you or never loved you, most of us are just dealing with life the best way we know how. You're not going to do that 25, they just need to get a few years out of you and let you go. Don't let those football numbers run a play in your mind. Remember you're from Harlem, we never lose, we always win, or learn."

While reading the letter for the hundredth time the following day, my focus shifted to the knock at the steel door that kept us encaged. Excitedly, my two roommates jumped up as if they were expecting someone significant. Oblivious to what was happening, I sat on the bed watching the interaction between them and the two ladies talking through the flap on the door. Immediately I was informed that these ladies one black, the other white, were part of a prison ministry organization that came by to preach the Word of God every Sunday. Looking up again, my eyes locked with the black lady, and she summoned me. When I reached the door, she just stared at me for what felt like an eternity. *What did she see?* She finally spoke and said,

> "You're not going to do the time man said, but God had to preserve you for a purpose greater than you can imagine. Your testimony is going to change people's lives, and you need to write a book. You can't cry

over spilled milk, so it's up to you to reverse the curse."

Deciding that I no longer wanted to be bitter, but better created capacity for the atmosphere to shift in my favor. Columbia International University extended its Prison Initiative Program to the ladies, after only providing it to men for the past six years. This allowed us to receive an Associate Degree in Biblical Studies with a concentration in Ministry. Acceptance was contingent on a contractual obligation to conduct three years of ministry duties at whatever institution you were needed. After the completion of all the necessary requirements, I submitted my application to the Chaplain's office.

Back at the dorm I sat on my bed reading one of my latest street novels by Ashley and JaQuavis. My brother was always on point making sure I had the latest literature, and this part in the book had my adrenaline pumping. There was a high-speed chase following a bank robbery, bullets flying, bodies dropping, and then out of nowhere a Scripture pops up, *Don't be misled, bad company corrupts good character (1Corithians 15:33).* This seemed rather odd and out of place. *But was it? Were my eyes deceiving me? Was God trying to tell me something?*

People are always watching, especially those you can't see. In the mailroom line, I was speaking with an associate recapping the highlights of a novel with all the dramatics. Suddenly, I was interrupted by a youth offender that was sweeping outside of the cafeteria. I had never held a conversation with this young lady but saw her around from time to time. Turning around to make eye contact she seemed distraught and asked,

"Hydessah, did you just curse?"

Instantly mixed feelings of emotions reverberated through my soul. As I analyzed the disappointment on her face, I began to question myself. *What did she see in me that I could not see? Why did she believe that I was beyond reproach?* We were all in prison, everybody cursed, but she had never heard me, until then. In that moment, her vision of me became distorted, but God

BLOOD AIN'T THICKER

would later give me the opportunity to make it clear again.

Following a strenuous interview process, I matriculated on a journey of educational escalation, and spiritual formation through Columbia International University. God has a unique and sophisticated way of revealing His Truth within the Scriptures. Honestly, the Bible was a complicated comprehension process comparable to deciphering the colorful configurations of a kaleidoscope. It didn't take long to experience a revolution of my soul and the Word became a composition of enlightenment enriching my life. Suddenly, I began to gain spiritual eyesight and became oblivious to the extraordinary events transpiring before my eyes. Vision becomes clearer when your lens gets adjusted. Instinctively, seasons that were once used to countdown the time have a greater meaning. Winter bemoans underdevelopment, Spring articulates cultivation, Summer celebrates innovation, and Autumn relishes harvesting the rewards of past labors. I suffered a wailing Winter before I could ever envision a spectacular Spring.

Mary said she was tired as we were walking from the cafeteria on Thanksgiving Day 2015. We developed a strong bond after her favorite counselor, who everyone said was my twin, left the institution. Cooling down from my workout, she asked if she could walk with me. From that day I was one of the few people who was able to cool her down. She would tell me that when she got out, she was going to buy a Lexus, pick me up, and drive everywhere. Mary had no support, so my mom started sending her money orders enabling her to get what she needed from time to time. She was a 5'2 powerhouse who would tear a dorm apart if provoked. On many occasions, I was called by the administration to calm her down, ensure that she took her medicine, and maintained a somewhat healthy diet.

After being incarcerated for over 30 years, Mary was getting tired of fighting knowing she would never make parole due to her mental health status coupled with the severity of her crime. Then she realized that I would be shipped after my graduation and expressed how painful it was to watch those she loved leave and forget about her. That Thanksgiving day we were in the officer's

BLOOD AIN'T THICKER

station of her building, and she collapsed. Suddenly everything seemed to be in slow motion the officer was panicked, medical took forever, and I held her, hugged her, and begged her to get up. But she was tired of fighting, so she decided to go to sleep forever. I was broken again. *Will pain forever be my portion?*

Amidst spectacular Spring, I graduated from CIU and was shipped 2 1/2 hours away to fulfill my contractual obligation of ministry work under the Chaplain. I created curriculums for personal development courses, hosted Bible studies, and mentored women one-on-one. God still had more and afforded me the liberty of helping the blind see by transcribing textbooks into Braille in an effort to further their education. Four months upon graduation, I joined the Braille Production Center and shortly afterward received my Literary Braille Transcriptionist Certification through the Library of Congress, specializing in Nemeth and Science. I could've never imagined that being sentenced to 25 years was a necessary consequence for God to cultivate the characteristics needed for the next phase of my journey.

HOLLI TABREN

Prior to my incarceration, I had a microwave mentality, and I realized my cousins' testimony didn't put me in prison, they were tools essential to planting the seeds of patience, which were watered with hope, and blossomed into faith. Now it's crockpot season and simmering slowly in solitude solidified my spiritual evolution. Originally, I had a solid brick fortification guarding my heart, mind, and emotions. Eventually, God's boulders shattered my brick wall as if it were a glass window. Then he started building a magnificent structure within me: my pain was cemented with promise, my despair was painted with destiny, my fear was carpeted with faith, and my hate was waxed with healing. Currently, I am still under construction however, it's evident that true healing derives from brokenness. One thing for certain, God was all I had during those midnight hours when my soul cried, and God was all I needed.

> "Attention in the area, attention in the area, the dayrooms are now open,"

was the announcement blowing through the speakers.

BLOOD AIN'T THICKER

Immediately I went to the phone to advise my family that we were no longer on lockdown. Before the call could be accepted the officer called my name, so I hung up and headed in her direction.

> "They need you to pack up and head to the administration building before count. Are you getting shipped?" She inquired. I replied, "No, I'm going home."

After serving 9 years, 8 months, and 11 days in one of the darkest places of my life, I finally get to see.

HOLLI TABREN

ABOUT THE HEART

The power that you possess is placed in the depths of your heart. Even when it's ripped apart, it adopts the personality of the liver when necessary and regenerates itself because what lies within can never be broken.

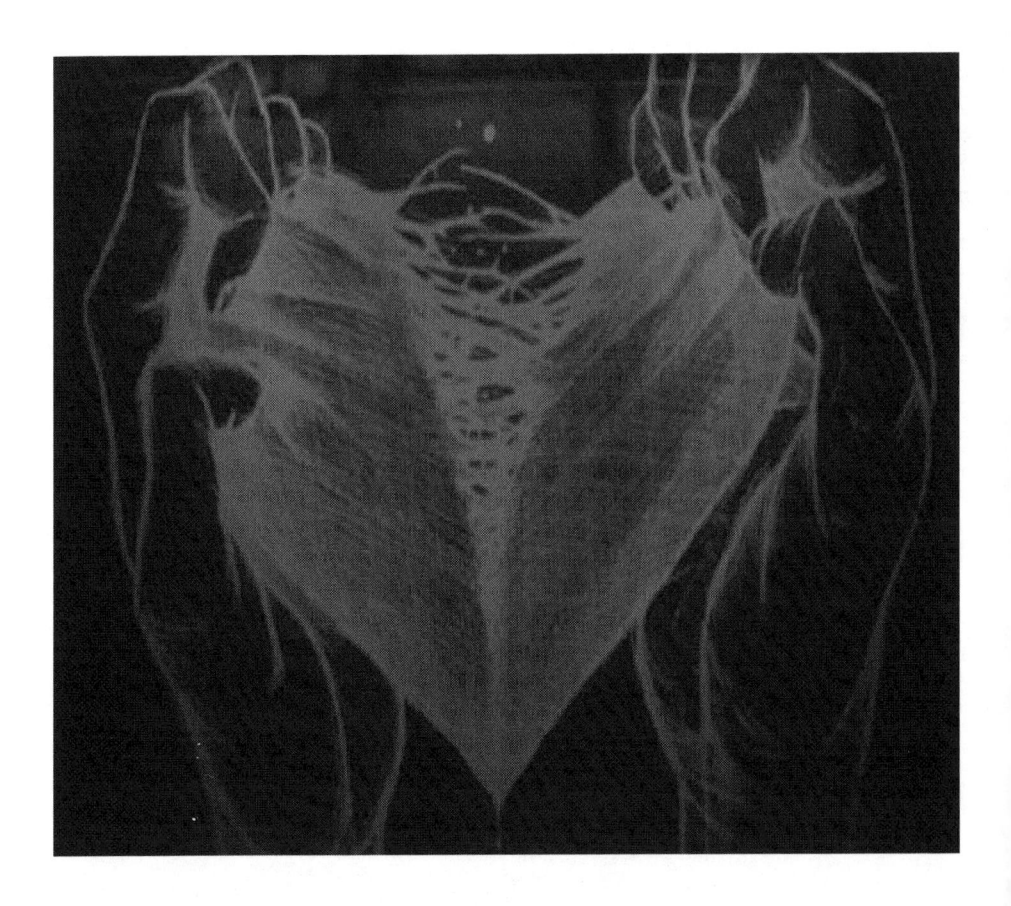

Made in the USA
Columbia, SC
06 March 2024